MW00576211

EXECUTIVE

SEVERANCE

Robert K. Blechman

Illustrations by David Arshawsky

NeoPoiesis Press, LLC

NeoPoiesis Press
P.O. Box 38037
Houston, TX 77238-8037

www.neopoiesispress.com

Text Copyright © 2011 by Robert K. Blechman
Illustration Copyright © 2011 by David Arshawsky

All rights reserved. No part of this book may be used or reproduced in any manner whatsoever without express written permission from the publisher except in the case of brief quotations embodied in critical articles and reviews.

Executive Severance by Robert K. Blechman
ISBN 978-0-9832747-5-9 (paperback : alk. paper)
        1. Fiction : Mystery & Detective. I. Blechman, Robert K.

Printed in the United States of America.

First Edition

This Twitter novel is dedicated to to my mother, Eugenia Blechman, who conveyed to me her love for Perry Mason mysteries and to the memory of my father, Milton Blechman, who I blame for my sense of humor.

Special thanks to Lance Strate and Dale Winslow for conceiving and pursuing the crazy notion from a publishing viewpoint that "Twitter Novel" is not an oxymoron.

And finally, thanks to my wonderful family, Alexander, Jess, Sara, Eliana, Peter, Rebecca, Henry, Philip, Peggy, Paul, Barbara, Richard, Grant and Lisa for putting up with the rantings of a would-be Twitter novelist these past few years, for your support and everything else you do! I love you all! Seriously!

Contents

Preface: Confessions of a Would-be Twitter Novelist

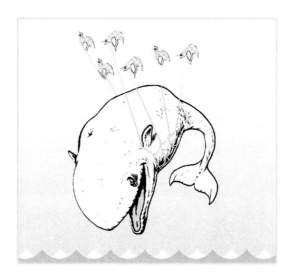

"What could be more practical for a man caught between the Scylla of a literary culture and the Charybdis of post-literate technology to make himself a raft of ad copy?" (169 characters) -Marshall McLuhan, *The Gutenberg Galaxy*, p. 77

According to Wikipedia, the Twitter network began in 2006 and as of this writing in 2010 is approaching 200 million users worldwide. (133 characters) By 2009 I realized Twitter was a happening thing and if I didn't jump on the bandwagon I'd be left behind with my ocarina and tambourine. (137 characters) But how to proceed? I had dabbled in Facebook and MySpace, but this Twitter thing was different. (136 characters) Limited to 140 characters (or less), with no photos, videos or extended links,

Twitter conveyed the brief, the inconsequential, the trivial. (140 characters) In other words, the Twitter medium was a perfect vehicle for my literary aspirations. (85 characters)

I conceived a literary experiment: Was it possible to maintain a narrative structure and attract a reading public 140 characters at a time? (139 characters) After 15 months and the more than 800 tweets that make up this Twitter novel, I can say confidently that the answer is "no." (125 characters)

I adopted the detective genre as the driver for my story because the murder mystery is such a standard part of our popular culture. (131 characters) Would my hero solve the crime? Would he undergo physical and mental trials? Would he get the girl? Would he spawn a publishing franchise? (137 characters) I soon realized that Twitter forced me to adopt the serial techniques of newspaper comic page story telling. (108 characters) To succeed I needed to learn and adopt the narrative strategies of Al Capp or Milton Caniff as well as Raymond Chandler or Mickey Spillane. (139 characters) How did comic strip authors hold their readers' attention each day and tell a joke while moving the story forward? (114 characters) How did mystery writers plant clues to direct or misdirect their readers while inexorably leading to the revelatory climax? (123 characters)

I created a new Twitter account "RKBs_Twitstery" as a container for my novel and coined a new term for the Twitter mystery genre. (129 characters) Starting on May 6, 2009 I posted a new *Executive Severance* tweet twice a day every day for 15 months, never missing a deadline. (127 characters) The 140 character limit required intensive wordsmithing, creative editing, the omission of punctuation in some cases and a lot of counting. (139 characters). I cultivated brevity, concision and obsessive-compulsion. Fortunately, once I completed my writing I was able to leave these habits behind. (139 characters) The cumulative result of my Twitter efforts is collected in the volume you hold in your hands. (94 characters).

Robert K. Blechman 2010

Chapter 1

The Twitstery Begins

Willum Mortimus Granger was beside himself. In fact when his body was found the top half was right next to the bottom.

Granger's body was split in two. "Well, we can rule out suicide" said the coroner. "I rule out NOTHING!" I replied.

Self bisection was not at the top of my list of likely solutions. I hate ceding any ground when it comes to crime deduction.

"Maybe this was self inflicted. Then how do you explain the 3 1/2 other victims just like this I have at the morgue?"

So Granger wasn't the only one cut down in his prime. "You said 3 1/2 victims. You have half a body?" "No. Siamese twins."

Willum Mortimus Granger and 3 1/2 others (as per the coroner) were dead, their bodies sliced in half.

I stared at Granger's lower torso. Marshall McLuhan famously claimed that the wheel was an extension of our feet. Now I got it!

Granger had owned a perfume concern, a blue coal mine and two pickle factories. His company was called Lavender Blue Dilly Dilly.

Hit hard by the economic downturn, LBDD failed the smell test, couldn't sink to new depths and finally everything didn't go sour.

A cloning pioneer, Granger had replaced every part of his body. Calling his lab 'Body Parts R Us', he was literally a self made man.

If the economic downturn had hit Granger's cloning lab, Body Parts R Us, like it did at LBDD, he could have lost an arm and a leg.

I knew a lot about Granger. By chance I'd just read his NY Times best-seller "100 Things You Need To Know About Me Before I Die"

"I was born at a very young age." begins Granger's autobiography, 100 Things..., "I was very close to my mother at the time."

Born to a family of neo-vegans, Granger ate only oats 'til age 17 when he became the first entrant to win the Kentucky Derby without a horse.

A self-taught fly fisher, when Granger discovered the sport's purpose was to catch fish, he released the flies back into the wild.

I looked at Granger's severed torso. Here... and here lay the remains of an entrepreneur, athlete, scientist and podcast mime.

Sure he was a failed entrepreneur, uncertain athlete, questionable scientist. But he was undeniably a world class podcast mime.

Who can forget Granger's podcast masterpiece, "Man Walking Against the Wind"? Or "Man Trapped in an Invisible Cube"?

Now he was ready to perform his final mime podcast "Man Silent as the Grave." Placing my cell next to his torso, I ...

pressed RECORD. Willum Granger was dead because, despite all his advantages, he couldn't be in two places at the same time.

We stood a moment in a respectful silence which the doctor broke asking "How can you do mime in a podcast?" Just then my cell rang.

Granger's last podcast would be ruined! I scooped up my cell wondering when I uploaded "Torn Between Two Lovers" as a ringtone.

My own phone was strangely silent. By the time I pried the other cell phone from Granger's cold dead hand, the music had stopped.

Looking for Caller ID I saw two things: Granger had been on Twitter at the moment of his death and the battery was almost dead.

Granger had been Tweeting when he died! This phone was the Holy Grail, the Rosetta Stone, the Jeopardy Daily Double of this case.

If Granger tweeted his assailant's name, or some clue, I'd wrap up this case and tackle those 3 1/2 other victims at the morgue.

If Granger wrote "Hey, Larry from LBDD! What are you doing here?" Or "Saw Vince from the lab" Those would be a definite leads.

Granger had married twice, divorced 3 times. His last wife had been really, really mad at him. Perhaps a she would be fingered in a Tweet.

I needed to know three things. What was the motive for the murder? What was the method? What was this stuff I just stepped into?

"What is this stuff, tapioca?" "No," said the coroner "That's his spleen." "It looks just like tapioca." "Believe me, it's not."

Doc's words reassured me. Tapioca always turns my stomach. Wiping my shoe on Granger's shirt, I tapped the phone on with my pen.

As the phone came to life the coroner scoffed "Do you seriously believe you can solve this case by following Granger on Twitter?"

"I won't follow his tweets to learn where he'll be. I already know with grave certainty where he's going to be from now on."

"I'll solve this murder not by tweeting forward, but by retweeting backward," I hit ENTER and Granger's final Tweet appeared:

aaaaaaaaaaaaaaaaaaaaaaaaaaaaaaaaaaaaaaaaaaaaaaaaaaaaaaaaaaaaa
aaaaaaaaaaaaaaaaaaaaaaaaaaaaaaaaaaaaaaaaaaaaaaaaaaaaaaaaaaaaa
aaaaaaaaa

aaaaaaaaaaa

Either Granger wanted his followers to know he suffered an extremely slow, painful death, or his finger got stuck on the "a" key.

"aaaaaaaa...?" said the coroner. "That's it?" "It may be a code of some kind." I replied "All I have to do is figure out the key"

The coroner continued, "Facing imminent death, as a final act Granger logs onto Twitter and tweets 'aaaaaaa...' to his followers?"

"Does that description do justice to the scenario you're painting here?" "Maybe we should look at his next-to-last tweet."

The coroner was getting on my nerves. I should put him on my suspects list. Once again I tapped the cell to view Granger's tweet:

"Stomach unsettled" Granger had tweeted, "I guess that tapioca didn't go down well." I glared at the coroner. He just shrugged.

The lab team was done and wanted to put Granger into body bags. His phone too. There wouldn't be another tweet out of either.

Chapter 2

Beeing and Non-Beeing

Granger's second wife was a beekeeper. "I still go by my ex-husband's name." she said shaking my hand. "You can call me Willum."

We met in a beeviary. Around us was the humming of a million bees. "I'll turn off the air conditioner" she said "So we can talk."

Willum's name was Rachel. I knew this because I had read the pre-nup. Rachel could only be Willum for two years after the divorce.

The drop-dead date was this week but Granger dropped dead ahead of that and "Willum" was up for grabs. Was Rachel a name dropper?

Mrs. Granger's maiden name was Lehcar. Never odd or even, Rachel Lehcar wed Willum Granger took his names and shed her palindrome.

Live was I ere I saw Evil. History is full of people who killed to make a name. Was Rachel's palindrome name a motive for murder?

The humming stopped. Without the air conditioner noise I noticed that there weren't any bees. Or they were beeing very quietly.

Rachel returned to the Beeviary. "Where are all your bees?" I asked. "I don't know" she replied, "I've had trouble keeping them."

"I'm here about your ex-husband's death" "What! He's not dead!" "Maybe not but they're taking the liberty of burying him Friday."

"I'm surprised you didn't know." I said "Didn't you get his last tweet?" "Yes. I thought his finger just got stuck on the 'a' key."

"Do you know how he died?" "You're the detective. Don't you know?" "I can't tell you." "Well, I haven't got a clue." Aha! A Clue!

If Rachel didn't know how Granger died, that would imply that she didn't kill him... Unless that's what she wanted me to think.

I needed to probe further without revealing how Granger died. "Could the press you use to process your honey cut a man in two?"

"You're thinking about winemaking. We don't use a press in beekeeping." "Then the power saw you use to cut up the honeycombs?"

"That's lumbering. I use a steak knife to cut the combs. It couldn't cut anything but wax." I didn't know much about beekeeping.

I tried another tack. "If you were the killer, you might say you hadn't a clue to get me to think that you weren't the killer."

"There isn't much here that could be used to kill. Maybe killer bees, but as you can see…" She gestured towards her empty hives.

"How horrible! Willum was cut in half." How did she know? "Do you know what killed him?" "We believe it was the cutting in half."

Rachel sat down. "Being cut in half wouldn't even slow down a man like Willum Granger. Something else must have killed him."

"Assuming you are right, and that the sum of Granger's parts was greater than the whole, what then could have brought him down?"

"Outside of general entropy, I can't think of a thing. Oh yes. He was allergic to bee stings. That's the reason we separated."

"I was administering bee vitamins the day Willum gave me his ultimatum. He asked me to choose between beeing and non-beeing. "

"I couldn't not bee, not even for him." she sighed. We sat in the eerie silence a moment. "I've often not been on a boat." I said.

"Someone more sophisticated may have chosen differently. Our relationship after that remained platonic." "Now he's a has-been."

Rachel glared at me. "Even cut in half Willum Granger is twice the man you are." She said. "Especially cut in half." I replied.

"Which is preferable, a whole man who may be half or two halves of a man who is double?" "You make both halves of my brain hurt."

"Its obvious you still have feelings for Granger. Why divorce him twice?" "Well they had a BOGO sale at the courthouse that day."

A 2-for-1 divorce followed by a 2-for-1 murder. So Granger's cutting her off led Rachel to cut him off. "And so you killed him."

"You do this for a living?" Rachel asked. "I had no reason to kill him. He gave me this Beeviary and a generous settlement."

"What about his name? You admitted that you still go by 'Willum'. You knew that 'Willum' would have reverted to Willum this week"

"Killing Willum wouldn't get me 'Willum'. His Will stipulates the name goes to his hares." "Don't you mean 'heirs'?" "No, hares."

"Willum left his name to the rabbits who test shampoos at his perfume concern. They'll institute cruelty-free product testing."

"With the proper Will, the proper name and the proper will, millionaire 'Willum' hares will end their at-will harassment."

"So Willum's Will wills 'Willum' to hirsute hare heirs harassed to harvest hair soaps?" "Yes. In a manner of speaking."

"Would you be willing to repeat that in a court of law?" 'I'm not sure I COULD repeat that in a court of law."

"Why did Granger stimulate his hares?" "You know that his perfume concern, blue coal mine and two pickle factories all failed."

"Yes. Lavender Blue is in the red." "Willum wanted to be eco-friendly and to turn Lavender Blue Dilly Dilly into Lavender Green."

"First, the renamed rabbits would exploit their new legal standing to quit the shampoo testing business for good."

"After the last hares split, Willum planned to shutter the coal mine. He just had to figure what to do with all the canaries."

"How about the prospect for his prime pair of pickle processing plants?" Rachel quickly held up her hand "They were green enough"

"You should talk to Willum's business partner, BJR." "BJR? What's his full name?" "That is his full name, just initials." "Why?"

"Perhaps his parents lacked imagination. Maybe they were lazy." "No, why should I talk to him?" "Oh. Because he's looting LBDD."

"What do you mean, 'looting'?" "I'm sure BJR is wetting his beak at the perfumery and getting his hands dirty in the coal mine."

"And he must have double dipped at the pickle factories." "How could you tell?" "He smells like black orchids marinated in brine"

"For someone who has been separated for two years, you seem to know a lot about Granger's affairs and his possible adversaries."

"Despite our problems we remained Facebook friends and mutual Twitter followers. Willum also helped when my bees disappeared."

"First he crossed my bees with homing pigeons so they could find their way home. Sadly, the pigeons found the bees delicious."

"Then he imported New Zealand bees theorizing that they would be immune to whatever GPS malady afflicted our native bee breeds."

"That worked until we discovered that the New Zealand bees produce toxic honey. We tried to get around the problem with a label:"

"'WARNING! Ingesting this honey may cause vomiting, delirium, giddiness, stupor, coma and violent convulsions.' Sales suffered."

"Our regular bees can tolerate the New Zealand honey, so we saved the entire output to feed to the hives over the winter."

Rachel showed me a side room where the honey jars each had a skull and crossbones label. "One of your jars is missing." I said.

"This room is full of honey jars. How can you tell one is missing?" "Simple. The jars are numbered and jar number 5 is not here."

This was an important development. Whoever took the honey jar may be Rachel's bee-napper as well. Why else steal toxic honey?

Jar number 5. The number of the jar taken might be an important clue. Perhaps the thief was using the number 5 to send a message.

"Wait" said Rachel "#5 is over here." "OK, it's out of place. So the missing jar is #47." "No. Here's 47. And here are two #178s."

How was Rachel going to get her bees in a row if she couldn't get her jars in a row? I made a bee line over to the last shelf.

"I don't understand it" said Rachel, "The last time I was in here, everything was in order, and all the jars were in sequence."

"Someone scrambled the numbers to mask that they took one of your honey jars." "I don't understand why they went to all this trouble."

"I'm not at liberty to reveal my suspicions. All I can say is that whoever took this honey probably took your bees as well."

"No one took my bees. All the hives are here. They just didn't return. It's been happening all over. Haven't you heard about it?"

I didn't know much about beekeeping. There was something else I needed to know. "Do you know Granger's Twitter ID and password?"

"His Twitter ID and password? Why do you need that?" "Granger was tweeting when he died. Maybe he tweeted his attacker's name."

"His ID was 'wgranger.' I don't know his password but I'll bet BJR does." "Why do you say that?" "BJR was Willum's ghosttweeter."

"There is such a thing as a ghosttweeter?" "Yes. Willum was often too busy to Tweet for himself, so he had BJR ghost for him.

"Didn't you just accuse BJR of theft?" "Yes, but BJR has eliminated all vowels from his speech, so he's a natural Tweeter."

"So LBDD COO BJR, who you call a con artist, and who converses only in consonants, conspired to contradict Twitter conventions?"

"Time to turn the air conditioner back on." said Rachel. "Please find your way out." "One thing more. Where were you last night?"

Rachel flipped a switch and the humming of a million bees filled the Beeviary. "Out." She replied. "Searching for my lost bees."

Chapter 3

Autocide

Decedent Willum Granger's ex-wife claimed that an extreme severance package would not have pink-slipped him.

But could I trust a would bee-keeper who couldn't keep a bee in her bonnet? There's a difference between beeing and knowing.

I was on my way to Granger's partner, BJR at LBDD. Granger's ex also said there was something shady there, but I couldn't see it.

LBDD headquarters were housed in a pair of classic Frank Lloyd Wright towers. BJR's office topped the left-hand Wright tower.

As I stepped on the brake I met no response. Someone had drained my brake fluid! Then the steering wheel broke in my hands.

With a sheer fatal drop mere inches away, the right front tire blew out. The car shuddered violently and the top wouldn't go up.

Since when did I own a convertible? Then I realized the truth. This wasn't my car. Someone had booby-trapped the wrong vehicle.

It was a good thing I hadn't started driving it yet. I wondered who would go to such lengths to kill the owner of this car.

As I puzzled over this I reached under the dashboard and yanked out the wiring to defuse the explosive device fastened there.

I stepped out and surveyed the compromised car. This auto-overkill was reminiscent of Granger's murder. Someone was very thorough.

Even more thorough than I had originally thought. The car made a popping sound and fell apart. I had just saved someone's life.

I couldn't wait around for the car owner to show up, so I put a note on what was left of the windshield: "You're welcome."

Someone was willing to resort to autocide to impede my investigation. I checked my own car over carefully before driving to LBDD.

As I drove out to the LBDD compound I went over in my mind what I knew for sure about this case. Fortunately it was a short ride

Item #1: Willum Granger was dead, cut in two. #2: He tweeted as he died. #3: If life is short, being cut in two makes it shorter.

#4: Limited to 140 characters to confess sins and meet his Maker, "tweeting" may not have been the best use of his final moments.

Still, Granger's last tweets were my only solid lead in this case and BJR may know the password that unlocks his Twitter history.

Chapter 4

Wright and Wrong

I pulled into the lot under the shadow of the Frank Lloyd Wright towers and went into the left-hand Wright building on my right.

Passing the out-of-order sign on the prairie-inspired elevator, I climbed 17 flights, admiring the stairwell's lily pad décor.

After a brief pause at the Native American oxygen inhaler at the top landing, I entered the waterfall cantilevered vestibule.

As I hopped off the last lily pad, I was greeted by a young woman. "Why didn't you use one of the other elevators?" she asked.

Changing the topic, I pointed to the water flowing down the lily pad stairwell. "Quite a marvel" I said. "How so?" she asked.

"Only Frank Lloyd Wright would incorporate a natural waterfall into his design." "He didn't. That water is from a burst pipe."

"Well, the lily pad design of the stairwell is quite unique." "Yes, if it wasn't for the frog infestation…How can I help you?"

"I'm here to see Mr. BJR about the Granger murder." "Who?" "BJR." "Do you mean Mr. B?" "I thought his name was BJR." "It's B Jr."

"Mr. B's office is in the right tower." "I'm in the Wright tower." "This is the left tower. You're in the wrong Wright tower."

"You erred by parking in the left Wright lot and by entering the left Wright tower. Two left wrongs don't make a right Wright."

"I was told B Jr works in the left Wright tower." "That's wrong. If you go to your other left you will be in the right Wright."

"Ask for Mr. B's assistant, Mr. X." "Mr. X?" "His younger brother. Mr. B was second of 26 siblings, each given a letter name."

"B has 25 brothers and sisters?" "Yes. It was the largest recorded simultaneous live birth." "Caesarian?" "No... Roman Catholic."

"That is a big family. So instead of naming one of their 26 children Lisa, for example, the parents just used letter 'L'?" "Yes."

"Do they all work for LBDD?" "No. Some are in children's TV. K went into Czech literature. M and Q work for British Intelligence"

"V is for Vendetta. W is in fashion publishing. A and B worked for the deceased. Some of the remaining letters are superfluous."

"A and B both worked for Granger?" "Yes, and of course my X works for B." "I'm sorry. Which letter was he?" "My X?" "Yes" "X."

"You used to be with X?" "He's still my X." "So you're no longer together?" "Yes we are. If we weren't together, he'd be my ex X"

We stood in water ankle deep. I had left my waders in the car. One doesn't often experience flooding at the top of a skyscraper.

Frogs croaked in the stairwell. Time to delve further. "So your boss goes only by the letter B?" She laughed. "He's not my boss."

"I couldn't work for B. He speaks only in consonants and swears like a drunken sailor. My non-profit rents space in this tower."

"We're an organization dedicated to protecting whales." "A noble cause. It's a crime the way they've been hunted to extinction."

She laughed again. "Not that type of whale. We protect Twitter fail whales." "Twitter fail whales?" "They are at serious risk."

"I thought the fail whale was a just some drawing Twitter displays during a system overload." "That's a negative whale image."

"A more positive fail whale image is of a mass of commercial tweeters trashing Twitter tweeting to too many other re-tweeters."

"Huh?" "What would you rather have: A passive whale of a Twitter network harpooned by its own inadequacies, held aloft by birds?"

"Or an active aggressive whale of marketing Tweets crashing through the structural inadequacies of Twitter's network bulkhead?"

I studied the famous crash drawing: A flock of orange birds hoist up a smiling white whale. "It seems that the Twitter whale fails upwards."

"Exactly" she said "he fails through his own actions, not due to some passive inadequacy. That's why he's smiling." I was missing something.

"Either way, Twitter crashes, spammers perish and followers are shut out." "Yes." She replied. "So causing Twitter to fail is a good thing?"

"Its a matter of interpretation. Is the social network half empty or half full? Evidently the Twitter administrators can't figure it out."

"Like the Twitter fail whale and the Twitter administrators, we must all rise to our level of incompetence. We must all fail upwards."

She continued, "We call our pro fail whale nonprofit 'Management Of Business and Youth Directed Interpersonal Communication Knowledge' "

I wasn't sure if it was our strange conversation or the fact that the water was now up to my knees, but a chill suddenly ran up my spine.

"You're M.O.B.Y.D.I.C.K?" "No, its 'Management Of Business and Youth Directed Interpersonal Communication Knowledge.' We don't do acronyms."

"But your organization is an institutionalization of and celebration of The Peter Principle. You're supporting the Great White Fail Whale."

"Yes. The Twitter fail whale and Herman Melville's whale tale are both about resolute, epic mismanagement leading to catastrophic failure."

It was time to get back on track. Was any clue to my murder case embodied in our exchange about fail whales? "You're still M.O.B.Y.D.I.C.K."

"And it was Melville who wrote 'There's no success like failure and failure's no success at all.'" "No. That was Bob Dylan." "Dylan?" "Yes."

Cascading water made the stairwell impassable, so I pressed the down elevator button. "Don't forget to speak to my X before you see Mr. B."

"Who should I say sent me?" "I'm Brynhildur Cathedra." "If you marry will you be Brynhildur X?" "No. We intend to hyphenate our last names."

The hall was flooded. I don't know why the elevator worked. For that matter, I didn't have any idea where all that water was coming from.

I turned to say goodbye to Brynhildur Cathedra but she had returned to her office. Maybe next time I saw her she'd be Brynhildur X-Cathedra.

As I left the left Wright building I was met by a phalanx of reporters. "Do you have a statement on Willum Granger's murder?" one shouted.

"If you all lower your spears and shields we can talk." "Is it true" one reporter asked "that Granger's death was gruesome and humiliating?"

"How would you define 'gruesome and humiliating'? Some might think being cut in half tweeting on your cell phone fits the bill. Not me."

"You know I can't reveal the cause of Granger's death or what he was doing at the time. But I can say a lot about Willum Granger, the man."

"Willum Granger was a man among men. He was also a man among women. He started each day with a song and ended each day with a lullaby."

"When Granger entered a room people stopped what they were doing. When he left they got back to work. World statesmen sought his advice."

"Religious leaders turned to him for guidance. Complete strangers asked him for money. To each and every one he said the same thing."

"ACHOOO!" The chill I felt earlier had progressed into a full-blown cold. A reporter asked, "Is that 'achoo' with two O's or three?"

"Three. I don't dow whad Grabger tode them, bud they all lefd dissadisfieb. ACHOO!" The reporters stared at me more blankly than usual.

In spite of my increasing cold-related symptoms, I continued. "So donb ask be about gruesomb abd hubiliatig. I belieb Grabger died a hero."

"He gabe his libe so others could lib. Don't ask be how. I'll take questions dow." A reporter stood up. "HL Menkin, Baltimore Sun." he said

"It is rumored that Granger's death was especially ironic. Any comment?" "Grabger libed libe on the edge. He also died on the edge. Dext."

"IF Stone, Independent. Is Granger's death a refutation of the military industrial complex?" "Grabger was a ban of peace and died in pieces"

"Mary Baker Eddy, Christian Science Monitor. "Given the premise of a benign diety, how do you explain the existence of evil in the world?"

I knew the answer to that one, but before I could speak others started calling out. "What was he wearing when he died?" "Who was he seeing?"

How did these reporters find me? I felt a sneeze coming on. "God is a shoud in the streed. He was wearing a cud-off. He saw his murderer."

"Are we talking about the same Willum Granger?" a reporter asked. "The one who was cut in half?" "We aren't sure about the cause of death."

It was time to end the press conference. "I hab tibe for one last guesdion." A reporter raised his hand "Do you validate parking tickets?"

As I stamped parking tickets I thought about my next step. I was a little hoarse and I felt a colt coming on. Still, I had to confront B Jr.

B's sordid reputation made him a prime suspect. Were Rachel Lehcar's allegations true? And what about the speaking only in consonants?

How could you navigate the rocky shoals of conversation without vowels? Still sniffling, I finished with the reporters. "Thag gue ebrywond."

Chapter 5

Lavender Blue Dilly Dilly

The right Wright tower was a duplicate of the left Wright Tower. An "Out of Order" sign adorned the elevator. Water poured down the stairs.

To my surprise a woman the exact twin of Brynhildur Cathedra stood in the lobby. I thought "Man, Frank Lloyd Wright was good…and demanding!"

"This is abazig!" I said."You bust be a twid." "Oh, you've caught a cold!" She said "And you've come back into the same Wright tower."

"So I'b ib the righd dower?" "No, you're in the left tower." I didn't want to start that again. "Leds dot sdart thad agaid." I said.

"You don't know your left from your right. Go home." "A code can't slow be dowd. I'll pull byself together. That's bore thad Gradger can do."

It was easy to mistake one Wright tower for the other. Outside they were the same. Inside the second tower I perceived subtle differences.

Wright's left tower had been arboreal, all natural stone and wood. His right tower was more of a cathedral. Less prairie and more prayery.

I entered the chapel-like LBDD lobby. On the crest above the door was a coal lump shaped perfume bottle resplendent on a field of pickles.

Diffuse light from a translucent ceiling spilled through open windows. I blew my nose and the sound echoed back from the far stone wall.

Along somber walls decorated with religious images and LBDD product displays ran the corporate motto "Mechanization Best Serves Mediocrity."

A statue I took to be of B Sr., LBDD founder, stood before me. If true to life, B Jr.'s father had been over 17 feet tall and well endowed.

The horns sprouting from the statue's head gave me pause. "Is thad your founder, B Sr.?" I asked a man standing nearby. "No. That's Moses."

"Boses founded LBDD? Your compady is older thad I thought." "It's a copy of Michelangelo's Moses used in our ads to sell perfume to seniors."

"Michelangelo's statue of Moses was part of our 'Scents and Sensibility' campaign that attempted to link smelling good to moral precepts."

"How did thad worg oud?" "We found that often when people wear perfume it is not their intention to embrace what we call moral precepts."

"Even with perfume brands like 'Eau de Nile,' 'Serenity by the Buddha' and 'JC's Eternity' the 'Scents' campaign was a biblical disaster."

"Awash in a million gallons of perfume, we drowned in a red sea of ink, failed to achieve reincorporation and went to hell in a bucket."

"We applied for a government bailout, but they thumbed their noses at us, claiming constitutional separation of church and scents issues."

"So your perfube busidess stingks. But whad's with the hords on Boses?" He looked at me. "You are here about Mr. Granger's murder." He said.

"You're Brydhildur Gathedra's X." "No we're still together. Brynhildur alerted me to expect you." "Achoo!" "You have a cold." "You doticed."

"Moses has horns because the ancient Hebrews didn't use vowels." "Huh?" "The description of Moses Michelangelo used was mistranslated."

"The original text described Moses having 'rays of light' coming from his head, but without vowels it looked like the Hebrew word for horn."

"I dond ged id." "Its simple. The same combination of Hebrew characters could mean 'rays of light' or 'horns' depending on how its read."

"Michelangelo's Moses has horns because of a pun in written Hebrew." "I ged thad. Bud why did you thingt a hordy Boses would sell perfube?"

X stared open-mouthed as I continued. "What's afder hordy Boses? Priapig Buddha or Ghrist risig agaid?" "You're conflating sects with sex."

"Our perfume campaign was the opposite of sexual exploitation. Its goal was to raise people's noses out of the gutter, Of course we failed."

X headed for the elevators. "We should go to see B. My brother has a very tight schedule." "I'b sure he'll hab tibe to adswer by guestiods."

"I'm afraid you won't get any answers from my brother." "Whads he hidig?" "Nothing. He won't understand you and you won't understand him."

"Begause he dalgs in godsodadts?" "What?" "He doesd't use vowels." "Yes." "Will you be there?" "I wouldn't miss it for all the tea in China"

"But there are do D's in 'Chida.' "X just looked at me and smiled. I needed to know more about B. "Why doesd't your brother use vowels?"

"There are two reasons why B won't use vowels. First, he believes that what was good enough for the ancient Hebrews is good enough for him."

"Id worged oud well for Bicheladgelo." "Second, B grew up second of 25 lettered siblings." "And five of them were vowels?" "Sometimes six."

"A, our oldest brother, became an MD. Other siblings got BAs, PhDs, f451s and other degrees. I myself dropped out of college my senior year"

"B had no proclivity for further letters. Barely finishing high school, B started his business career selling pots and pans door to door."

"B was a salesman's salesman. He just couldn't sell to anyone else. Failing in kitchenware, he also went bust in ladies' undergarments."

"B claimed he could sell refrigerators to Eskimos and lost a fortune in appliances. When he tried to sell doors pot to pan B Sr stepped in."

B's death as a salesman didn't explain his peculiar way of talking. "Wad does thad all hab to do with speaging odly in codsodadts?" I asked.

"B speaks in consonants because of a fight he had with A. It had to do a terrible mistake made during Mr. Granger's last organ transplant."

It was well known that Granger had replaced nearly every organ of his own body through his cloning lab 'Body Parts R Us.' What went wrong?

"A was Chief of Medicine at 'Body Parts R Us.'" "And B Jr. thought Gradger's accidedt was reasod to elibidate all vowels frob his speegh?"

X ignored me. "As I said, A and B had a terrible fight. Blood was drawn. Some of it was completed in oil, others remained just sketches."

"As reviews by medical art critics were generally Rh negative, the A-B antagonism was surpressed." "Id becabe a segred blood feud." "Yes."

"It came to light when the other vowel siblings sided with A against B." So the bloody feud between A and B was revealed by a vowel movement

Granger's cloning mishap turned brother against brother, consonant against vowel. Was it also a motive for murder? And on whose side was Y?

"Thad's why B abjures vowels. X, which side did you take?" "I first joined A but then I double-crossed him." "Why?" "Because its my nature."

A gruesome murder; tweeted clues; missing toxic bees; failing killer whales; consonants forsaking vowels. This case was becoming complicated.

"My brother is often misunderstood. I'll act as interpreter." "So whad was the fighd aboud?" "Let's let B tell you himself." X said smiling.

X pressed the down elevator button. "We're dot goig to the pedthouse?" "B's offices are in the tunnel tower beneath us." "The tuddel tower?"

"We built LBDD Tower over our blue coal mine. When we lost the lease above we created a duplicate office tower in the empty tunnels below."

"You built a duplicade tower in a coal mide?" "Yes, a carbon copy except its only 3 floors." "Thad's dot a tuddel tower, thad's a basemedt."

Chapter 6

Notes from the Discordant Underground

The elevator arrived. X handed me a hard hat with a light and a cage with a canary inside. "You can keep the canary afterwards." he said.

As we descended I heard a loud buzzing. "Whad's thad doise?" "You can't smell it? Our unsold perfume storage vats are on the first level."

"I hab a code," I said "I ca'd sbell a thig. Whad's that budzing?"
"All that perfume attracts millions of bees. We can't get rid of
them."

We arrived at the third level. If the motif for the upper floors was
"prairie office" the layout before me might be "subterranean
prairie."

Tunnel Tower indeed! Stretched before me as far as the eye could
see were offices and worker cubicles carved out of the depleted
coal seam.

Of course in the dark the eye couldn't see very far. LBDD Inc in
extremis had gone underground horizontal, eliminating the room
with a view.

The original mining rail connected the 'bottom' of the tunnel tower
to the 'top." "Where is B?" I asked. "He's in the executive shaft."

The coal car started down the mine. Nestling the bird cage on my
lap, I asked X, ""If all your worgers are dowd here, who is id the
tower?"

"We leased our LBDD Tower space to companies that are still
financially viable; insurance carriers, lobbying firms and internet
startups."

So the once proud firm of Lavender Blue Dilly Dilly, Willum
Granger's vast industrial empire, was reduced to this trifling
carbon footprint.

The train stopped at a large, ornately carved wooden doorway. X opened the door to reveal an office suite built directly into the bedrock.

A broad shouldered man sat at a large desk. He looked up at us from his computer and said "Wh th fck s ths sshl?" "B says 'Welcome'" said X.

"He said 'Welcobe'?" "Yes" "Whad aboud the rest?" "Rhetorical flourish" said X. "Wht's hs fckng prblm?" asked B. "He has a cold." X replied.

"Yr fckng tllng m tht ths mthrfckng ccksckr brght hs fckng cld dwn hr t sprd rnd?" "Whad he say?" "He says he's concerned about your health"

I could see that this interview would require my utmost subtlety and finesse to be successful. "So, how's the ebbezzlig busidess?" I asked.

"WHT?" said B. "Afder all, you liderally drobe LBDD idto the groud. Was thad why you killed Willub Gradger, to hide your cribe?"

"Bllsht! Dn't hv tm fr yr fckng nnsns!" I looked at X. "B is a no-nonsense kind of guy" I said "You'll tage my dodsedse and you'll lige id!"

"FCK Y!" "UB YOURS!" "Wht?" "Whad?" "Gentlemen, please calm down!" said X "It's clear that what we have here is a failure to communicate."

"You're wrong about my brother embezzling us into ruin. LBDD is bankrupt due to his ruthless and unrelenting mismanagement not malfeasance."

X continued "You give my brother entirely too much credit. B is just not capable of the complex financial manipulations you ascribe to him."

X was probably right. After all, what sort of idiot decides to make his speech patterns all but incomprehensible due to a family argument?

B released his headlock and I let go of his jacket. "Do hard feeligs." I offered my hand. "Kss my ss" said B "nd kp yr fckng grms t yrslf."

"B is goonish and ill-spoken," X concluded, "but not criminal." "Y cn pss n my mngmnt" said B "bt ths dpshts dtctng rlly scks hgh n th tt."

"Whad he say?" "B compared his managerial acumen to your detecting prowess." Not rising to the bait, I decided to let B goons be B goons.

"Led's stard over. I'b idvesdigatig Gradger's death. I hab sob guesdions for you ad yes, I hab a code." "Wll fck y nd th hrs thrt y rd n n."

I didn't get much of that. Something about my hoarse throat. "Do you ever ged gridicized for usig profadidy so graduidously?" "Sht ys."

Something about B was unsettling. I knew him from somewhere else. Hadn't I seen his likeness at the post office or maybe in a police lineup?

I realized that B was the spitting (and cursing) image of Willum Granger, only younger, heavier, with a different nose, chin and a monobrow.

And while B's hair and eye color, skin tone, body type and skull phrenology were all different his resemblance to Granger was still uncanny.

Had there been a tragic mixup at the artificial insemination lab all those years ago when B and his 25 letter siblings were conceived?

Did they discover a DNA match during Granger's recent transplant? That could mean that Willum Granger, not B Sr, was B Jr's father! Nooooo!

But if Granger sired B Jr and his 25 siblings, why not join him and rule the LBDD empire together? What kind of man kills his own father?

Looking at B and X, I couldn't imagine a baser pair. What were A, T, G and C like? Their dark DNA secret caused the phonetic family feud.

Perhaps being in the coal mine so long was playing tricks on my mind. I checked my canary who slept peacefully at the bottom of its cage. OK

Even if there was an ancient family curse which doomed B to commit patricide and to marry his own mother, that was no excuse under the law.

For now I decided to keep my suspicions to myself. I looked around B's cavernous office. "So" I asked, "Adythig Oedible aroud here?"

"This is an office at the bottom of a coal mine" said X, "The only thing I can offer you is coke" "No Pepsi?" "Y thnk ths s fckng Grk dnr?"

"Fair edough." X set a lump of coal in front of me. "Led's assube for the sage of argubedt you gilled Gradger, dot dowig he was your fader."

B and X both stared daggers at me. Undaunted, I continued. "Ad led's assube thad you thed barried your buther id ad irodig turd of evedts."

Both men jumped up. "ARE YOU OUT OF YOUR MIND?" shouted X. "Y MTHRFCKR!" yelled B. "Agtually, I'b wodderig if you are the buther fugger."

Screaming incoherently B lunged for me. X had to restrain him physically. I opened my coat to expose the holster I wear under my left armpit.

I wish I had remembered my gun. Instead I had a cell phone with a "virtual gun" application. I took aim and pulled the virtual trigger.

B's cell phone chimed. He stopped his assault and took it out to read the text message sent from my phone's virtual gun ap. "BANG!" it read.

B stopped dead in his tracks. I pointed at X. ""I hab ad idchy virdual trigger fidger. Dod't bage be text you too." They both sat down.

Stuffed up as I was, it was clear that B and X had no idea what I had just said. That didn't matter. I was the one holding the virtual gun.

"Wht dd ths sn f btch sy t y?" "He said 'Don't make me text you too.'" "N sht?" B put his head in his hands. I blew my nose and continued.

I needed to know three things. Where was B when Granger died? Why did he fight with his siblings? What was this stuff I just stepped into?

"Whad is this stuff, tapioga?" Looking up B said "That's ambergris. It comes from whales." "It loogs like tapioga." "Believe me, it's not."

"We used to use it to make perfume. Now we use synthetics derived from coal or oil." B's words reassured me. Tapioca always turns my stomach

I realized that B was speaking normally! "You're speagig dorbally!" "Yes. You've made me see that effective public speaking is important."

"I understand how hurtful obscene language can be and I recognize the perils of speaking without vowels." "Really?" "Words have power."

"We live in an environment where communication media determine what we say, think and do. We shape a 'media ecology' and then it shapes us."

"Bud you were Gradger's ghosttweeter because you dod't use vowels." "Yes. Now I can separate speaking from tweeting. Form dictates content."

"Huh?" I said. I admit that even though B seemed to be speaking normally, I understood him even less than when he 'spoke in consonants'.

I looked at X. "B is saying that as we pass from secondary orality to secondary literacy, we must be aware that the medium is the message."

Now I couldn't understand X either. Twitter was the only medium I was concerned with. Most tweets were tedious. The tedium was the message?

I'm almost certain Twitter is not so tedious as death. The grave's a fine and private place, But none, I think, do there embrace. Or tweet.

Granger had spent his last moments tweeting and probably would be tweeting still were it not for roaming charges. Was tweeting his te deum?

Whether out of tedium or a te deum, Granger's terminal tweeting was still central to my investigation. I needed his Twitter password.

I felt hot and cool at the same time. I couldn't tell if I was shedding light on or light through my case. It was time to marshal my wits.

Just then a young woman came in. "Sorry to interrupt. Did you find the bowl of tapioca that was sent to you? I left it there on the floor."

I glared at B. He just shrugged. Wiping my foot on the rug, I asked "Who sent the tapioga?" "The note just said 'Enjoy! Signed, Anonymous.'"

I turned to B. "Do you ofted receive gifts of tapioga adodybously?" "Hell no" he replied, "I thought it was an anonymous gift of ambergris."

"Gradger ate sumb tapioga pudding just before he died. It wedt right through hib. If by suspiciobs are correct, I just saved your life."

"From pudding?" "Do. toxic hodey. Do timb to explaid. I deed to dow Gradger's Twidder password." "Why?" "I believe a follower gilled him."

"This goes to the lab for adalysis." I put what was left of the tapioca in my pocket. That was a mistake. I should carry evidence bags.

"I'll write down Granger's password." "You cad't just tell be?" "No." B spent several minutes writing and thinking and thinking and writing.

He handed me the paper which read:
'Ullhodturdenweirmudgaardgringnirurdrmolnirfenrirlukkilokkibau gimandodrrerinsurtkrinmgernrackinarockar."

"This is Gradger's password?" "Yes. He believed in using complex passwords." "You're dot gidding." I slipped the paper into my pocket.

"I hab two guestiods. Firsd, where were you Tuesday dight?" "We were here, working." "Were there witdesses?" "Is that the second question?"

"Do. Id's a follow up to the firsd questiob." "Several staffers were with us, testing our surplus perfume for use as a pickling agent."

"We're developing sweet smelling pickles. The black orchid half-sour smells promising." "Good lug with thad. Whad did you ad A fight aboud?"

"Why do you need to know why we fought?" "X told be there was sub terrible accidedt durig Gradger's last clodig tradspladt." "Yeah, so?"

"Ad that's whed you becabe so adgry at your siblings you stopped usig vowels." "So what?" "Dod't you thidg it a bit extrebe?" "Not at all."

"You know Granger funded 'Body Parts R Us' to commercialize on cloning technology and he replaced nearly every part his own body." "Yes."

"The economic downturn hit us all hard. With funding constrained, Body Parts R Us began cutting more than just corners." "Whad do you bead?"

"There's a lot of our DNA that scientists can't identify yet." "Uh huh." "The lab rats at BP'R'U just decided to leave those base pairs out"

"They used cut-rate DNDA?" "Granger thought he was getting cloned when in reality he got spliced. The cloners took him to the cleaners"

"So you fought with A ad the other vowels because they were cheatig Gradger by shortchadgig his DNDA?" "No. I didn't care about that."

"Whad bothered you?" "Granger wasn't paying for services provided. You pay plastic surgeons a lot for a little nip and tuck, right?" "Sure."

"We gave Granger the equivalent of a DNA liposuction—without charge. BP'R'U didn't want it to come out. I wanted to send him another bill."

"You said BP'R'U toog hib to the cleaders." "They also did his shopping and walked his dog. They provided many concierge services for free."

"Were there side effects frob the DNDA splicig?" "Not to speak of." said B. "That's not strickly true." said X. "Granger complained a lot."

"Granger wasn't himself after his last brain transplant." "Well, he had a dew braid afder all." "He claimed they mixed up his hemispheres."

"Granger complained his left side was seeing left and his right side was seeing right." "Odly his left side was affected?" "No, both sides."

"Whad differedce does it mage which hebisphere is where?" "It makes a big difference." said X "Different sides control different abilities."

"The right processes images and spatial orientation. The left controls the three 'R's, reading, writing and 'rithmetic." "Whad happeded?"

"With his left and right hemispheres switched, Granger couldn't tell his 'R's from a hole in the ground." "Did he have any other problebs?"

"He complained that his kidneys were put in backwards and his bowels were shaped like a klein bottle. He was a man under a lot of pressure."

"To sub up, A switched Gradger's braid hebispheres, screwed up his idterdal plubbing, redacted his DNDA ad you wadted to bill hib for it?"

"Hey, Granger put his pants on just like the rest of us, one leg at a time." "Dot ady bore." "Well, he should pay for services rendered."

"Subthig I still dod't udderstad. You create perfube frob coal tar idstead of whale vobit ad you wadt be to eat cucubers soaged in it?"

B looked surprised. "If I were you I'd question A about Granger's murder. He had motive and he had means." "A did't do it. I thidg you did."

"That's crazy!" ""Too bad you did't realize thad before you gilled hib." "You think I killed Granger?" "You are by dumber onde suspect."

"Why?" "Gradger would have kept A's secrets to protect his cloding lab. You hab a better chadce of collectig your bill frob his estate."

"You lost your fight with A and your cobpady is in the toilet. Gillig Gradger puts you on top at LBDD with Gradger's cash in your pocget."

"You suspect me after my proper speech and contrite demeaner?" "Yes" "And my alibi and the tapioca?" "You could hab sedt thad to yourself."

"WLL THN FCK Y Y SSHL!" Consonants again? I looked at X. "B says you'll have to speak to his lawyer from now on. And you're an asshole."

"How do I kdow B wod't go uddergroud whed I leave?" "He already is underground. I'll show you out." "Dod't bother. I cad fid by owd way."

As I made my way to the door B sneezed several times. "GD DBBT!" He roared "V CGHT YR FCKG CLD!" "Gesudheit." I called over my shoulder.

Chapter 7

Auto-Erraticism

12 hours later, reeking from perfume, covered in bee stings, ravenous and in serious need of a bathroom, I emerged from LBDD's Tunnel Tower.

There's a time in every criminal investigation when you should stop and smell the roses. I needed to stop because I smelled like roses.

Time to head home. I thought my car was missing but soon realized that it was still in the left Wright parking lot, right where I left it.

As I drove home I thought about how all the pieces had fallen into place. B's 'perfect' alibi of perfumed pickles was patently preposterous.

B knew that Rachel Lehcar would never miss one jar of her honey and that the coroner would overlook the tapioca in lieu of the severed body.

B lured Granger to a remote spot, fed him toxic honey-laced tapioca and cut his body in half. It all made sense. It was the perfect crime.

Except B forgot one thing: Granger was such a Twitteraholic that he would try to tweet a dying message. It was too bad he didn't succeed.

I had Granger's Twitter password. There still might be something to find in his online account. I pulled the paper B gave me from my pocket.

Tapioca in my pocket had gotten onto the paper, smearing most of B's writing. The letters left read 'murderir b not.' What did that mean?

My cell phone rang. With the tapioca soaked paper in one hand, I fished the cell phone from my holster while driving with my elbow. "Hello?"

"Want a tip on Granger's murder?" asked a husky voice. "Who is this?" "Got a pencil and paper?" I put the phone between my ear and shoulder.

Pulling a pad and pen from my jacket, I said "Go." "Have you got a voice recorder?" "Yes." "Take it out. You'll want a recording of this."

I put the pad and pen in my mouth and fished out my recording device. "OK." "You'll need a computer to view a website I'll give you."

My opened my laptop and set it on my lap. "Ready." "How are you at multitasking while driving?" said the voice. Not so good it turned out.

Chapter 8

How Can You Be in Two Places at Once When You're Not Anywhere at All?

I woke in bed in a dimly lit room. I was in a hospital gown, hooked to an IV. A bandage was wrapped around my head. "Where ab I?" I asked.

A man came in. "You're awake! You had us going for a while." "Whad happeded?" "You were injured in a cell phone induced traffic event."

"A whad?" "Many people experience a sort of tunnel vision when they talk on the phone while driving. It's called 'inattentional blindness'."

"I thoughd thad odly cabe frob basterbating." "Not exactly. Its clear that human consciousness is affected by doing too many things at once"

"You were on your cell, your voice recorder, your laptop; you had a pen and pad of paper in your mouth. You went into a multitasking fugue."

"You then attempted parallel universe parking. Your mind left your body and you tried to park in two different spots at the same time."

"Ad thad caused by head idjury?" "No. The guy you cut off from the second parking space got out of his car and clocked you a good one."

It was becoming clear to me that I had been set up. "It's luggy I wasd't pilotig ad airplade." "Yes. You might have ended up in Milwaukee."

"The good news is your car suffered minor damage. The bad news is you yourself may need some new parts. Fortunately, that's what we do."

"This is Body Parts R Us?" "Yes." "Let be speag to A." "A? He doesn't work here anymore. You also appear to have a head cold. Drink this."

I downed the clear bubbly liquid. My sinuses cleared and my cold was completely gone! Except for my slight concussion I never felt better!

"Amazing! Was that some new experimental antiviral medication? "No. Alka-Seltzer Plus. If you lie back down, we'll prep you for surgery."

"Wait. What are you operating on?" "You can't see it, but the accident made a terrible mess of your face. We can help." "Let me have a mirror."

I looked at myself in the mirror and didn't see anything different. "What are you talking about? This is how I've always looked." "Sorry. My mistake."

"I had a run-in with a swarm of bees. It will heal on its own." "If you say so. We still can help with your little problem..um, down there."

I pulled the sheet up higher. "What little problem? I don't have a problem. It's cold in here." "I was referring to your ingrown toenail."

"My toenail?" "Yes. What are you talking about?" "Never mind." "You know, we can help you there too. We get a lot of requests of that type."

"We started 'Body Parts R Us' to clone internal organs and enhance lives. It turns out most of our business comes from enhancing penises."

"We also replace breasts, thighs and wings. All our work is guaranteed. If you don't like your new part, return it for a full refund."

"Maybe some other time." "If not a larger penis, how about something hepatic? We have a blue plate special today on liver and bunions."

"I could slot one in for you at a very attractive price." "My liver is fine." "Our prostates are big, I mean normal size but popular."

"I'm very happy with the prostate I have." "We also do vasectomies." "No." "Tell me, what will it take to put you in a brand new model you?"

He leaned closer. "Help me out, will you? I need to meet my monthly quota." "I'm not here to be cloned. I'm investigating Granger's murder."

"Bring me my clothes so I can get out of here and make some arrests." He looked at me sheepishly. "I'm afraid I can't do that." "Why not?"

"I thought you'd be in surgery. Your clothes smelled like you fell in a vat of black orchids marinated in brine. I sent them to be cleaned."

"What about my things?" "Your cell phone, a sticky piece of note paper and what looks like tapioca are in the drawer next to your bed."

"I'm afraid your canary died." "He's just sleeping." "If you say so. I found him 'sleeping' under the right front wheel of your car." "Oh."

"What killed him?" "We think it was the car on top of him. We did find traces of tapioca in his beak." "Look Doc" I said "I've been set up."

"Someone wanted me brought to Body Parts R Us. They got my canary and I'm next." He laughed. "I'm not a doctor. And you're quite safe here."

"Nobody can get into Body Parts R Us without proper credentials. You don't need to worry." "You're not a doctor?" "No. I'm your concierge."

"This is a world-class hospital and a secure, cutting edge research lab. No one and nothing gets in here without our knowledge. Period."

There was a knock on the door. A teenage boy entered the room "I have an order for a large pizza and side of tapioca for room 414." he said.

"You have the wrong room" said the concierge. "This is 441." "You can leave the pizza." I said. "No. We don't allow outside food."

He turned back to me. "My job is to manage your stay and approve your payment options." "Just send any charges to my insurance company."

Another knock. A young woman leaned in and asked "Can I interest you in an assortment of money saving coupons?" "No." said the concierge.

"How do they get in here?" he said. I watched the woman leave. "I thought this was a secure location." "Well, no system is 100% foolproof."

"We submitted a bill to your insurance. Your multitasking-induced mental fugue was deemed a preexisting condition and payment was rejected."

A tall man walked in. "I'm a Nigerian prince." he said. "I'm happy to inform you that room number 414 has won $800,000 in the lottery."

I frowned at the concierge. "I'll handle this." He said. "This is 441, not 414. You have the wrong room." "So sorry." said the man and left.

The concierge watched the Nigerian prince leave and then said, "Excuse me, I need to have a word with the security guard." "Take your time."

Outside I heard him hail the prince, asking "Are you happy with your current prostate?" I decided to make the most of my momentary privacy.

A small TV hung on a metal arm next to the bed. Unfortunately, service had not been switched on. All I could get was a children's channel.

Running on a continuous loop on the children's channel was an animated version of something called "Goldie Dinosaur and the Three Bears."

"Once upon a time" said the GD & 3Bs narrator (who sounded like Morgan Freeman) "there was a beautiful little house at the edge of the wood"

"Inside the house lived three bears: the Papa Bear, the Mama Bear and Baby Bear. One morning Mama Bear made hot porridge for breakfast."

"The cereal was too hot to eat, so the Bear family decided to walk in the woods until it cooled down." This story seemed strangely familiar.

"As the Bears disappeared into the woods, Goldie Dinosaur appeared on the path." A large reptile with long golden hair approached the house.

GD & 3Bs continued: "Goldie Dinosaur had also gone out for a walk before breakfast and the smell of porridge suddenly made her very hungry."

"Goldie Dinosaur meant to just take a small taste of porridge from one of the bowls, but she misjudged the size of the kitchen window."

"Smashing a huge hole in the wall, she swallowed all three bowls of cereal in one gulp, as well as the kitchen table and all the chairs."

"Her hunger now satisfied, Goldie blundered into the living room where a few ill-placed steps soon reduced the furniture to splinters."

"Now very sleepy, it only took Goldie Dinosaur a few short steps through the wall to where she discovered the Bear family bedroom."

"There was Papa Bear's large bed, Mama Bear's medium bed and Baby Bear's tiny bed. She lay down across all three beds and fell fast asleep."

This was somewhat different from the story I knew. The narrator continued: "At this moment, the Three Bears returned from their walk."

"Papa Bear regarded the large new opening leading into the kitchen and said, 'Somebody's been eating my porridge.'"

"Mama Bear looked at the empty space where the table and chairs had been and said, 'Somebody's been eating my porridge.'"

"Baby Bear looked at his parents. 'What are you talking about? There's a hole in our kitchen wall and our table and chairs are gone!'"

"The Three Bears entered the living room where they surveyed the damage. 'Somebody's been sitting in my chair' said Papa Bear."

"Mama Bear picked up a fragment of her favorite rocker. 'Somebody's been sitting in my chair.' She said."

"'I don't believe it!' said Baby Bear. 'Can't you see that all our furniture has been smashed to smithereens?'"

"Then the three Bears climbed through the new entrance to their bedroom. "Somebody's been sleeping in my bed" said Papa Bear."

"Lying across the broken bed frames, Goldie Dinosaur snored peacefully. 'Somebody's been sleeping in my bed.' said Mama Bear."

"'WHAT IS WRONG WITH YOU?' shouted Baby Bear 'THERE'S A HUGE GOLD-HAIRED DINOSAUR ASLEEP IN OUR BEDROOM!' At this Goldie Dinosaur woke up.""

"She was so frightened that she crashed through the wall on the opposite side of the bedroom, ran down the lane and was never seen again."

"The Three Bears decided to cut their losses. They put the house for sale as a 'fixer-upper' and went to work pushing paper products on TV."

The narrator concluded "What's the moral to our tale? Whether dinosaurs or banks or the Twitter whale, some things are too big NOT to fail."

Chapter 9

Goldilocks

I was watching "Goldie Dinosaur and the Three Bears" a third time when a blond-haired woman, also in a hospital gown, ducked into my room.

"I need your help," the blond said, "Someone has been sleeping in my bed." "One second." I said. On TV the dinosaur ate the kitchen again.

"That part always kills me" I laughed. "You're watching cartoons?" "It was that or 'Now You Are About to Give Birth' on an endless loop."

"I said 'Someone has been sleeping in my bed.' Doesn't that interest you?" "I'm not interested in the details of your sordid personal life."

The blond seemed as if she now regretted coming to my room. "If you're too busy, I guess I'll go back to my room and get it over with."

I looked at her for the first time. She was tall where she needed to be tall. The rest of her amply obeyed the rules of bilateral symmetry.

When she first came in I assumed she was just another hospital room spammer. Looking at her more closely, I realized that wasn't the case.

First, she was in a hospital gown which I had noticed before without really noticing. Second, she was bare foot. Third, she wore no make-up.

I needed to know three things. Why had she come to my hospital room? Who was sleeping in her bed? What was this stuff on my dinner tray?

"What is this stuff, tapioca?" "Yes," she said, "I believe it is." "It looks just like tapioca." I said. "That's because that's what it is."

Her words reassured me. Tapioca always turns my stomach. "You've got to help me" She said. "Why me?" "I was told you're a police detective."

"Yes. That's true. But as you can see, I'm tethered to this IV unit and I also have a catheter. I'm not going anywhere tonight."

"Those are no problem." she said. "What do you mean? Ouch." She had removed my IV line. "OK. That wasn't so bad. What are you...OOUUCH!!"

"OK. You're good to go." She said. "Wait." I turned around to examine the damage. "I may not be able to use this for a month." "I can wait."

"Huh?" "I mean, take your time, detective." "I think you've given me a second circumcision." "So now you're a born-again dick. You'll heal."

"What's your rush?" "I told you. Someone's in my room. Its room 414, right next door to you." "You can't be next door. This is room 441."

"The layout of the 'Body Parts R Us' facility is like a drawing that Frank Gehry crumpled up and threw away. So 414 is next to 441." "Oh."

"They're continually remodeling the BPRU facilities, so when we go out watch your head." "Who are you?" "My name is Regna. Call me Regi."

"And you are Detective Arkaby. I read your chart. Were you really brought in for double parking? I'd think a cop would have that covered."

"It wasn't exactly double parking. More like an out of car body experience. What brought you in?" "Do you mean, what am I having replaced?"

"Yes. From where I'm standing, you don't need anything replaced." "That's true. I'm here under false pretenses. I'm investigating a murder."

"What do you mean?" "Can you keep a secret?" "Sure." "Willum Granger was my father." "You're Regna Granger?" "Actually, Regna RG Granger."

"Your mother is Rachel Granger, ne Lehcar?" "Yes. How did you know?" "Not much gets past me." "I never would have guessed." "One question."

"What is RG short for?" "Just RG." Regi's name was also a palindrome. Perhaps Rachel Lehcar hadn't married Granger just to change her name.

I now knew the Granger family backwards and forwards. But how can you investigate a murder if you don't know whether you're coming or going?

Regi headed for the door. "I'm going," she said "Are you coming?" "I don't know. How can you investigate your own father's death?" "I must."

"I was content to leave it to the authorities until I saw the man they assigned to the case interviewed on TV." "You saw me, er, him on TV?"

"What an idiot. 'Granger was a man among men.' Really! I wouldn't trust that man to solve a jigsaw puzzle, much less my father's murder."

"Um..." "So if I want the murderer brought to justice, I'm going to have to do it myself." "Do you have any experience as an investigator?"

"Experience?" Regi said, "No, but how hard can it be? It looks to me like any idiot can investigate a crime." "You're too hard on yourself."

"Huh?" She stopped at the door and looked at me. "Your investigation has barely begun and you've already made three critical mistakes."

"How so?" "One of your mistakes was too hot, one was too cold and the last was just right." "What in the world are you talking about?"

"First, sneaking around in a hospital gown is way too hot." "Don't be ridiculous. This rag isn't flattering at all." "Speak for yourself."

"Second, you are way too cold about the lead detective investigating your father's murder. The man you saw interviewed on TV is me." "You?"

Regi came closer. "That's a bare-faced lie. You don't look at all like him." "I had a mishap with some bees at your father's perfumery."

"The swelling will go down on its own." Regi wrinkled her nose. "At any rate" she said, "that explains the almost unbearable flowery smell."

"Third," I continued, "you are just right in seeking help if someone is in your room. But why didn't you go to security or the floor nurse?"

"Due to cutbacks, the nurse is security." "That's why the spammers got through." "Yes. I figured a police detective would be a better bet."

"Even one who is himself hospitalized?" "If there's something grizzly waiting in my room, I figured you could always call for backup."

"And fourth, you're wasting your time. I've already solved your father's murder." "I thought you said I had made three mistakes." "I did."

"The third wasn't really a mistake. It was an observation." "You know who killed my father?" "Yes. He put me here to put me away." "Who?"

"B is the one." "You think B killed my father, B?" Regi started laughing. "Yes. To take over LBDD and to collect withheld concierge fees."

She laughed harder. "Wait, I have to catch my breath. You're talking about B, who fails at everything? That B?" "Yes. Why is that so funny?

"Uncle B, who tried to sell refrigerators to Eskimos? He's your prime suspect?" Regi wiped tears from her eyes. "You seem skeptical." I said.

"I'm sure the coroner's report will show that B did it." "I know one thing. If B had set out to kill my father, he'd still be alive today."

At that thought Regi grew silent. After gaining an inch or two she said "Come on. I still need you to bear witness to whoever is in my bed."

Regi disappeared through the door. Grabbing my phone with one hand and my crotch with the other, I followed her, moonwalking into the hall.

Chapter 10

Body Parts R Us

I entered a concave corridor stretching in both directions like the centrifuge habitat of '2001'. New construction was visible everywhere.

Regi said that BP'R'U was always being remodeled. I ducked under a scaffolding on my right to enter her room. That turned out to be wrong.

This wasn't Regi's hospital room. I was alone in a vast hall filled with medical exhibits. I stepped up to the first case and peered inside.

What I first took as a chronological depiction of the stages of human growth turned out instead to be a compendium of human abnormalities.

Before me floated a large headed fetus. Bobbing beside it, an infant with an exposed intestine. Across the way, a child with clubbed legs.

Further down was a person who had died with an advanced case of spinal curvature. I couldn't make out the contents of the farthest cases.

All the display cases were filled with similar examples of human deformities, abnormalities or afflictions. It was a museum of grotesques.

As I stood contemplating these mortal remains a hand fell on my arm. "Yikes!" I noted, jumping a foot in the air. "Yuk! What is all this?"

It was Regi. "Wait. Don't tell me." She pointed at the exhibit in front of us. "That's my nightmare tonight. That's my bad dream tomorrow."

She gestured towards the next case. "And that will haunt me for a month." She turned to me. "Did I startle you?" "No, the floor is cold."

"I thought you were following me to my hospital room." she said. "I was" I said, "I made a wrong turn." "I'll say. What is this place?"

"Let's find out." There was a computer in front of us. Following onscreen directions, I held up a card and a museum guide materialized.

"Hola!" said the Augmented Reality docent. "Bienvenidos a la Galería Genética del Museo de 'Partes del Cuerpo R Nosotros'."

"Wrong card." I held up the English card. The same AR docent said "Hello! Welcome to the Genetics Gallery of the 'Body Parts R Us' Museum!"

"We've gathered thousands of examples of human genetics for research and reflection." So there was a reason for the horrors in front of me.

"Why is that little man floating in the display?" asked Regi. "Its an augmented reality docent that's computer-generated from this card."

The AR docent continued: "The five displays are set around the theme 'Healthy and Sick'. Each display shows a specific phase of human life."

"I'll guide you through each display." If I turned the card sideways I found I could make the AR docent lie prone or stand on his head.

"Stop that!" the AR docent said. "Huh?" I dropped the card and he vanished. Regi went to the entrance. "Perfect. We're locked in." She said.

There was another door at the end of the gallery, just past the inevitable display of Siamese twins. "Maybe we can split that way." I said.

Gathering my hospital gown, I strode down the aisle and stopped short. "Regi, stay where you are. Maybe we should try the front door again."

"I'm coming down." Regi said. "No. Just stay there." I stood before a life-size statue of Willum Granger. It was an excellent likeness.

I read the inscription on the base of the statue: "This hall is dedicated to our founder, Willum Granger. Often duplicated, never imitated."

"My God!" Regi had come beside me. Floating in a display opposite his statue was Willum Granger himself. It was an even better likeness.

Chapter II

Hail Poetry!

This couldn't be Willum Granger. For one thing, he was in one piece. For another, the real Willum Granger was currently at the city morgue.

Regi stared in horror. "Is that my father?" "Of course not." said a voice. "Your father was cloned so many times we made a reference copy."

"The thample here inthured that our work doethn't become thloppy." said another voice. "You're doing it again." "Doing what my friend?"

"Following me in rhyme." "To thpeak in verthe ith not a crime." We turned to face a pair of life-sized AR docents. "Oh, You two." said Regi.

I held up my hand. "I'll decide what's a crime and what's not." "Who are you?" they said in unison. "I'm investigating Granger's murder."

"I thought the little man on the computer looked familiar" said Regi. "Are these also clones?" I asked. "No. This is Dr. Dot and Dr. Dash."

"They direct Body Parts 'R' Us." Dr. Dot was a small man in a dark suit with a bow tie. Dr. Dash wore a similar suit, but with a normal tie.

"They look enough alike to be twins." "We get that a lot." "But twinth we're not." "Stop that!" Dash just smiled. "Why are they doing that?"

"Dash thinks if he annoys Dot enough he'll quit and there will be only one head of Body Parts 'R' Us." "Well, he's certainly annoying me."

Regi was livid. She grabbed Dot and Dash by their neckties."You circus clowns have a clone copy of my father as an exhibit in your museum?"

"Your father was a brilliant man" said Dot. "A copy here wath hith own plan" said Dash. "Will you cut that out?" "You don't have to thout."

As Regi choked off further debate I whispered "We have not world enough and time for this. And your hospital gown is open." She let them go.

I needed to know three things. Why was A no longer at BP'R'U? Where was he now? What was that stuff Willum Granger's clone was floating in?

"What is that stuff, tapioca?" "No" said Dot, "It's a gelatin we use to preserve clones." "I wouldn't think clones make good preserves."

"Without the gel cloneth thoon decay to thkin and bonth." Dash's words reassured me. The thought of clone preserves always turns my stomach.

"You're co-directors of Body Parts R Us?" They nodded. "B felt two heads are better than one." "Tho he gave the lab to both of uth to run."

"I thought A was the sole Director." "A resigned after Mr. Granger's last surgery." "That'th not exthactly true. You're committing perjury."

"Why did A quit?" "Mr. G and A differed on the goal of human genetics." "It had leth to do with evolution thcienthe and more with etheticth"

"Genetic esthetics?" "Mr. G wanted to move to the next stage of evolution." "A didn't think that thith wath an appropriate tholution."

"He started with his stem cells." "From which he created thtencilth." I was lost. "Thtencilths what are thtencilths?" "Stencils. Templates."

"With each transplant we modified his DNA." "Improving the part we cloned in a thertain way." "Stem cell stencils? You tailored his genes!"

"Not tailored, but rescanned." "Cloneth make the thuperman." Regi asked "Can it be my father practiced self-eugenics?" "Quite." "Right."

"Only he knew how to move mankind higher." "And the amount of thpandexth it would require." Regi glared at them. "You're annoying me now."

With Granger's clone floating in aspic behind them, I surmised that naked people have little or no influence on society. Most naked people.

"Was Granger right?" "I'm afraid the final data needs further study." "Before man can fly through the air or thtretch hith body like putty."

My spidey sense tingled. Something about their story was amiss. I brushed the spider off my sleeve. "And A refused to go along with this?'

"We don't really know." "He left thome time ago." "WILL YOU STOP RHYMING ME?" "I don't think that can be." Dot was about to tackle Dash.

"So Granger used genetic esthetics to create augmented stem cell stencils of his own organs cloned to climb the evolutionary staircase?

"I believe that's what we said." "Are you thick in the head?" "Did you say sick or thick?" "Thick" "I'm not clear." "Thick! Are you thick?"

"I had a head cold but I'm better now, thank you. I was told Granger's transplants had gone awry and he suffered unintended consequences."

"There were some minor glitches." "In geneticth you exthpect thome hitcheth." "Hitches? You switched his brain halves and knotted his guts."

"Who told you that?" "Wath it the cat?" Dot turned to Dash. "That rhyme doesn't make sense at all." "Baby, that'th jutht the way I roll."

They stood nose to nose. Dot said "True wit is nature to advantage dress'd." "I don't care," said Dash "I jutht want to thee you thtreth'd."

Regi stepped between Dot and Dash. "Look, you odd couplet, I want my father's clone removed from that display." I motioned Dot over to me.

"If you tell me more about where I can find A, I'll tell you how you can get back at Dash." "I've told you all I know." "I don't think so."

"Now you're doing it." "Sorry." Dot looked over his shoulder at Dash who was in a heated discussion with Regi. "Can you show me some ID?"

"ID?" I was still in my hospital gown, but I had an idea. I held up my phone so Dot could see the photo of my badge in my Twitter bio.

"What are you showing me?" "This is my badge." "On your cell phone? What are you, a phony detective?" "No. A true detective who tweets."

"To whom do you tweet?" "To whoever follows me on Twitter." "You're a detective who tweets the truth to Twitterers you can't detect?" "Yes."

In the background Regi was hitting Dash with a computer keyboard. "OK" Dot said, "I'm going to tell you this in the strictest confidence."

"My lips are sealed." "Look for A in your own city morgue." "He's dead? Was he also cut in half?" "No, he's wholly alive. He works for you."

So A left 'Body Parts R Us' to work for city government. What unfortunate sequence of events could convince anyone to stoop to such depths?

"I'm confused about one thing." "Just one?" "B and A fought over charging Granger for concierge services related to his operations." "Yes?"

"Now you're telling me that Granger and A fought over the ethics of artificially induced evolution." "Not the ethics. The esthetics." "Huh?"

"Much of human DNA is in the form of a palindrome." "I didn't know that." "The base pair palindrome tells ribosomes where to cut and paste."

"Ribosomes?" "Ribosomes are components of cells that make proteins from RNA." "RNA?" "DNA copies itself to RNA which ribosomes can read."

"RNA is a semordnilap to DNA." My head really hurt. "What in the world is a semordnilap?" "Semordnilap is 'palindromes' spelled backwards."

"A palindrome is the same backwards and forwards. A semordnilap is a word or phrase that spells a DIFFERENT word or phrase backwards."

"For example 'deliver no evil' becomes 'live on reviled.'" "So ribosomes can read RNA semordnilaps, but they can't read DNA palindromes?"

"Do geese see God?" "What does that have to do with esthetics?" Regi came over. "I broke your keyboard" she said, handing the pieces to Dot.

"Where's Dash?" "Oh, he's laying around here somewhere. He's agreed to remove my father's clone." She looked at Dot. "Of course." he said.

"Mr. G wanted to rewrite his DNA as ALL palindromes. A said that showed a lack of understanding of genetics fundamentals. Then it got ugly."

"Is genetic code that accommodating?" "Of course not." Regi looked perplexed. "Why would my father meddle with fundamental laws of nature?"

"At his core he was an artist." "I thought Granger aspired to become superman." "He wanted his DNA to be both functional and constrained."

"Constrained?" "As in poetics. Mr. G wouldn't leave DNA to its own literary devices. You see the results." Dot waved toward the exhibits.

"A classic case of nature vs. nurture. A countered that genetics is not a stylistic device. DNA is code, pure and simple, not literature."

"I don't get it." "Their dispute became an irreconcilable conflict of form versus content. For Mr. Granger, the DNA medium was the message."

"I got that. The question was, who's the boss, Granger or his DNA. But why did A go to work for the city rather than into private practice?"

"Do you know what they call the person who graduates at the bottom of his medical class?" asked Dot. "What?" "Doctor." "Ah." "No, Doctor A."

"What is he doing there?" "I honestly don't know. Now tell me how can I stop Dash from rhyming me" "Just use a word that can't be rhymed."

"A word that can't be rhymed? Like what?" "Well, the word 'month' for example. There is no word that rhymes with 'month.'" "Really?"

"Try it." Dot seemed relieved. Dash came over, rubbing his head. "What did I mith?" "I believe Dr. Dot has something to say to you."

Dash look expectantly at Dot. Grinning Dot said "April is the cruelest month." Dash smiled back and said "You only have to thay that oneth."

Dot looked at me. "Poetry's not so bad, really" I said. "Augh!" he screamed and lunged for Dash. I took Regi's arm and headed for the exit.

Chapter 12

Speed Derrida

We left the BP'R'U Genetics Museum and found ourselves just outside room 414, Regi's room. "Well, that went from bad to verse," she said.

"You can't spell crime without r-h-y-m-e." "Do you suspect Dot or Dash?" "I think it's more likely your father was killed by his own clone."

"Was Granger always obsessed with palindromes?" "I don't know that he was." "Your name, your mother's name, his DNA?" "What about them?"

"All palindromes." "He never mentioned it to me." "I think that you are the living message Granger sent to a time he would not see."

"My father intended to live forever. Why would he send a message when he could deliver it himself?" "I was speaking metaphorically."

"Wouldn't it have been simpler if my father sent a message via the post office?" "You don't need a postman to know which way your kin goes."

"That's crazy talk" said Regi "Father lost faith in cloning and intended to close BP'R'U." "I can see why he'd want no further parts of it."

"This is my room" said Regi. "So it is. How is it we walked from my room, through the Genetics Museum and are now just outside your door?"

"I told you, this place is like a discarded Frank Gehry blueprint." "So room 414 is right next to 441 and also across the building?" "Yes."

"If I want to go to my room do I retrace my steps through the Museum?' "Or just go next door." "Does it matter if I go right or left?" "No."

This wasn't the first hospital I'd ever been in that needed a search engine to find your room. Regi crossed her arms. "Well?" she said.

"Does the layout bother you?" "Actually, this is my kind of place. How do I know I've found my room?" "I think you'd know your own room."

"And every room is numbered, of course." "But if the numbers aren't sequential, a random walk would work as well as an organized search."

"Better. Do you have your gun?" "Gun?" "To check out my room, remember?" "Right. I don't have a gun, but I do have my cell phone gun ap."

I showed Regi how gun ap worked. "So you send the text message 'BANG!' to the other person's cell instead of actually shooting them?" "Yes."

Regi studied the screen text for a moment. "What if whoever is in there doesn't happen to have a cell phone?" "Then I have the advantage."

"Advantage? How?" "I can call for help and he can't." "And if he has a real gun that goes 'BANG' and shoots you with a real bullet?"

"We're still talking about the guy sleeping in your bed?" "Yes, of course." "And this guy in your hospital bedroom is packing heat because?"

"It's true that normally a rich industrialist's willful, yet glamorous daughter would not be a target, but my father ran with a bad pack."

"I thought his horse racing days were over." "They are. My father was an internationally renown podcast mime." "So I've heard. What of it?"

"There is a secret international organization of podcast mimes. If he was about to betray them, they'd stop at nothing to silence him."

"They offered him hush money. When he didn't answer, they tried the silent treatment. His lack of response only heightened their resolve."

"As a bone fide podcast mime, wasn't Granger already speechless? And now that's he's silent as the grave, why are they coming after you?"

"I'm not saying they're after me. I'm saying there's someone in my room who could be a bald, speechless, albino, podcast mime assassin."

Having experienced Granger's mime podcasts, I understood the desire to silence him permanently. But would podcast mimes resort to Regi-cide?

I couldn't refute Regi while barefoot in the corridor. I was getting cold feet. Maybe her assassin did too. "We should peek inside." I said.

I opened the door and looked in. Sure enough, there was someone in Regi's bed. I closed the door and said "He's still there. I'm going in."

"Just be careful." said Regi. "Don't worry. I read your room with a single glance, like a good book." "You can read a book with one glance?"

"What I mean is to my trained eye details stand out in bold relief and obstacles are accounted for." "That's more like reading Cliff Notes."

"To read a good book you must savor the language, ponder the characterizations and descriptive prose and appreciate the dramatic structure."

"OK. A book was a bad metaphor. What I meant to say is that I scoped out your room with a single glance and formulated a plan of action."

"Which is?" "I told you. I'm going in." "That's it?" "I know everything I need to know to enter your room and disable whoever is in there."

"So what did a glance of your trained eye tell you?" "He's square shouldered, about 6'2" with a tattoo on his back. He likes anchovies."

"Anchovies?" "That was from his breath. He's expert in either the 42-line Bible or the Tianemmen scrolls. In the dark I can't tell which."

"He flosses regularly. He carries cash rather than plastic." "You could tell all this about him from one glance?" "Just the obvious stuff."

"Anything else?" "He gained admittance to Body Parts 'R' Us claiming he wanted to trade an ear for an eye. He is biased toward the visual."

"His lips move when he reads. He prefers Vermeer to Picasso. He is Machiavellian in his dealings." "Uh huh. So what are you going to do?"

"I'm going to slip in, disarm him if necessary and find out who sent him. You wait here." Regi studied me for a moment. "Go get him, tiger."

Like diabetes or atherosclerosis, podcast mime assassins are silent killers. Subduing him would take all of my speed, cunning and prowess.

I entered the darkened room, closing the door behind me. In the brief instant of light I saw that whoever lay in Regi's bed hadn't stirred.

I mapped out my moves, matching my mental map to the hospital room territory. In my mind, the bed was exactly 2.4 meters from the door.

Stooping to apply 70% peak force to my hip extensors, I'd leap on top of the unsuspecting mime, and land with an estimated impact of 24 PSI.

A swift punch at 35 PSI 3 cm to the left side of his jaw would fracture his mandible rendering him senseless. I'd need to secure his wrists.

A Spanish bowline tied with the sash of my hospital gown would serve. Then a search for weapons and his days of silent menace would be over.

I couldn't see a thing, but I had my mental map. Like a jungle cat just before it pounces, I knew exactly where I was and where I would go.

I bent down for my mighty leap. What I hadn't counted on was that I'd caught the hem of my gown when I closed the hospital room door.

Springing into the air, I left my gown behind and cartwheeled headfirst into the floor by the bed. I realized I needed to know three things:

Who was doing that moaning? Where was I on my mental map? What was the stuff in the bowl my head had plunged into? Please let it be tapioca.

The answers came to me. I was the one moaning. My mental map no longer matched the territory. The bowl contained tapioca. That reassured me.

The door flew open, washing the room in bright light. Regi entered the room, surveyed the scene and doubled over in laughter. I sat up.

"OK I fell. Can you hand me my hospital gown and a towel? If you wake the assassin you won't think it's funny." "That won't be a problem."

"Take a glance with your trained eye behind you." I turned around. There was no podcast mime assassin in Regi's hospital bed. Nobody at all.

A large pizza box with a map of Italy on top, a stack of money-saving coupons and what looked like piles of money formed a rough body shape.

Regi had been visited by hospital spammers. In the dim light she mistook spammer materials and the pizza box for a lurking podcast mime.

I also had jumped to conclusions. The printed pizza box became tattooed square shoulders. A thick stack of coupons seemed a Gutenberg Bible.

Scattered piles of money mimicked human arms and legs. A closer examination showed that only the anchovies were what they seemed to be.

All else was illusion. The coupons were only good with further purchases. The money was fake. The pizza was cold. I put on my hospital gown.

Regi sat next to me on the bed and wiped tapioca off my face. "Sorry I laughed. Thank you for helping me." She leaned forward and kissed me.

"Despite the outcome, I appreciate you believing me and jumping in on my behalf." "That's OK. I had to go in after the podcast mime anyway."

She studied my face. "Where did you fall?" she asked. "On the floor" I replied. "You know you have three of the bluest eyes I've ever seen."

"Uh huh. Maybe we should get you back in bed for a while." "It's a tempting offer, but I don't have time. I must get back to headquarters."

"Slow down, sailor. You may be concussed." "I'm fine." "Then why did you dunk your head in a bowl of soup?" "This isn't soup. It's tapioca."

"Tapioca? Then it all makes sense." "I didn't dunk. I plunged. What kind of soup do you think I'd dunk my head into?" "Noodle, of course."

Still a little shaky, I stood up. "I'm going back to my room to get dressed." "I'd feel better if you'd let me drive. I need a ride anyway."

"What happened to your car?" "It was mysteriously dismantled last time I visited my mother." "Well, the top wouldn't go up anyway." "Huh?"

I made my way to the door. "It's not general policy to let a civilian drive a police vehicle. I can make an exception this time." "Wait."

"How do you know my car's top wouldn't go up?" "I was there when your car toppled over. Whoever topped off Granger may be after you too."

"YOU left the note 'You're Welcome'?" This was a turning point in our relationship. It was crucial that Regi didn't misinterpret my answer.

"Yes." I said. "YOU'RE WELCOME?" "No need to thank me. I was in the right place at the right time." "YOU LEFT MY CAR A PILE OF SPARE PARTS!"

"Whoever killed your father was trying to kill you too. That is an important clue. I just got in the way." "MY BEAUTIFUL CAR...SPARE PARTS!"

As Regi savored the irony I realized something vital. Granger prolonged his life with spare parts. Regi's car had been reduced to the same.

Granger's killer was a "deconstructor." His modus operandi was to take things apart, to "deconstruct" his victims. I called up Wikipedia.

The Wikipedia definition said "Deconstruction is not a dismantling of structure, but a demonstration that it has already dismantled itself."

That made perfect sense. Deconstruction was not the same as destruction. All the killer had to do was convince Granger that he didn't exist.

Stripped of ontological certitude, Granger would disintegrate of his own initiative. No telltale clues would lead back to the killer.

After that, convincing Regi's car it lacked structure would be child's play. Or, the killer may have used a variety of automotive tools.

Here was the problem: By Wiki definition, the infinitely subtle ways the deconstructor worked his effects cannot ever be completely known.

If Granger was deconstructed, the killer somehow making him dismantle himself, logic suggested it might be impossible to solve his murder.

My investigation stood at a crossroads. On one side were a possibly unsolvable crime, an inconsolable daughter and an irreparable victim.

On the other side were a diabolical deconstructor, a hobbled investigator and a pile of automobile detritus. It was time to take a stand.

Regi picked up the pizza box and hurled it across the room. "CAR...PARTS!" she reiterated. "Yes, I know" I said, "But I'm not giving up."

"WHAT are you not giving up?" she shouted. Avoiding a flying anchovy, I ducked through the door. "My car keys, for one thing." I replied.

Chapter 13

Carpe Per Diem

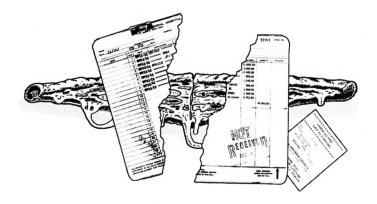

It only took an hour to find my own room where a $40,000 hospital bill awaited me. My dry cleaned clothes hung in the closet. My head hurt.

As I was dressing the Concierge came in the room. "$40K for dry cleaning?" I asked. "Not just dry cleaning." "I'd like an itemized bill."

"Certainly, for a small additional charge." "But you didn't do anything!" "You actually would have been better off had you chosen surgery."

"I would have been better off had you left me on the highway." I put B's tapioca sample and Granger's Twitter password in my jacket pocket.

As I examined the bill Regi knocked on the door. "I'm sorry I lost my temper" she said, "You weren't the one who dismantled my car."

"Miss Granger!" said the Concierge "Are you leaving us?" "I've changed my mind about augmentation surgery." "One thing bothers me." I said.

"In all the time I've been here I haven't seen a single doctor or nurse." "And?" said the Concierge. "That doesn't seem strange to you?"

"We've made cut backs." "You cut back on the doctors and nurses but left concierge services? How do you do surgery?" "We use per diem docs."

"So you discovered the real hospital money is in ancillary services, not medicine. You fired the permanent medical staff and hired temps."

"Nonsense." "Is it? It explains why Granger's recent surgeries were botched. He discovered what you'd done and objected, so you killed him."

"Mr. Granger was a regular client and the founder and benefactor of Body Parts R Us. Why would I kill the goose that laid the golden eggs?"

"B told me that Granger refused to pay for his concierge services. Regi just revealed that her father was considering shutting down BP'R'U."

"Finally, you killed him to collect your exorbitant fees from his estate." "An interesting theory. However, you've overlooked one thing."

"A performed all of Mr. G's operations not per diems. If anyone botched the surgery it was A." "What are you two talking about?" asked Regi.

"Mr. Arkaby suspects I killed your father but he can't prove it" "Really? Do you suspect me too?" "I'd suspect you if I thought you did it."

Regi made a face. "Is this about your hospital bill?" asked the Concierge, "Maybe we can reach an accommodation." "Here's my accommodation."

I tore up the bill. That shocked the Concierge. "You can't do that!" "I just did." "That wasn't your bill. It was a representation of it."

"You tore up a sign of your debt. Your bill remains." "Tearing it up was a symbolic act, symbolizing that I am not paying that bill."

"Why don't you suspect me?" asked Regi. "What do you mean?" "I'm his daughter. Why aren't I suspect?" The Concierge picked up the torn bill.

"You'll pay for this bill too" he said. "I just said I won't." "I mean for this actual bill. It costs money to print these things out."

"You want me to pay for the symbol of my debt as well as the sign?" "It would be a crime not to." "Crime doesn't pay. And neither will I."

"I'm really not a suspect?" said Regi. "I have no reason to suspect you." "But my father and I fought constantly!" "That's hard to believe."

"I had ample reasons to get back at him." "Get back maybe, but murder? Give me a break." "Um, your bill?" said the Concierge. "One minute."

"You don't think me capable of killing my father?" "No." "Well that's just ridiculous. I'm a more likely suspect than that idiot concierge."

"Hey! I'm standing right here!" "You keep out of this!" said Regi. "Let me get this straight." I said, "You're saying you killed Granger?"

"What? No! Of course not! I'm just saying I could have and I shouldn't be dismissed as a possible suspect." "Excuse me..." said the Concierge.

"WILL YOU WAIT?" Regi and I said. "I'll just let you two sort things out." Placing the bill scraps carefully on the bed, he left the room.

"How's this?" I said, "I'll add your name to my suspect list, even though you're not on my suspect list." "I still need a ride." said Regi.

"I can't give you a ride if you're on my suspect list." "You could take me downtown for further questioning." "That's good enough for me."

My head still hurt. By the time we found my car in the BP'R'U lot and combed it for any tampering my headache had become a raging migraine.

I could risk driving, enter a mental fugue again and wind up back in the hospital. Or, let Regi drive. Reluctantly, I handed her my keys.

"You can drive, but you must follow my instructions to the letter." "Alphabetically?" "No, literally." "Left to right?" "No, exactly." "OK."

"Don't play with the siren or flash the lights." "Right." "Don't talk on your cellphone, surf the web or write down notes at the same time."

"No multitasking. Check." "Don't fool with the GPS. It isn't working properly. And whatever you do, don't double park." "Got it. Get in."

Chapter 14

Carapace

Regi and I were on our way to Police HQ. My entire case rested on proving that the sample of tapioca in my pocket was the murder weapon.

While Regi drove, I went over what I knew about Granger's case. A run-of-the-mill human bisection had turned into a more complicated matter.

I walked an empty Scandinavian street   in   blinding sunlight.   I stopped under a big   clock with no hands. My pocket watch   also lacked hands.

My watch, being digital, wouldn't have hands anyway. A man stood on the corner. To my horror he looked like Robin Williams in "Popeye."

Robin/Popeye collapsed just as a driverless, horse-drawn hearse turned onto the street. The horses seemed to know where they were going.

The carriage bounced over a "sleeping policeman" in the road and two caskets in the hearse tumbled onto the street, popping open.

I leaned over the first casket. The top of Willum Granger reached up and grabbed my wrist. "Turn left in 100 yards" he whispered.

Granger's bottom half reached up from the second coffin and kicked me in the rear. "No, turn right in 100 yards" the bottom half whispered.

THUMP! It kicked me again. "NO!" said Granger's upper torso, pulling me closer "Do a U-turn at your earliest possible convenience!" THUMP!

I woke up. Regi thumped the GPS unit again."Vad skedd?" "Huh?" "What happened?" "You're Swedish?" "No. I sometimes dream in Ingmar Bergman."

"Why are you hitting the GPS?" "This thing keeps changing its mind. It won't tell me which way to go!" "I told you not to use it." "Why?"

"It has a dual persona and sees as through a glass darkly." "All I get are cries and whispers! What about principles of global positioning?"

"The only principle this GPS box operates under is the uncertainty principle." "Well, I think it should learn to operate outside the box."

"In my dream both halves of your father operated outside the box. His top half was no better than this GPS, and his bottom half kicked me."

"You dreamt about my father?" "I don't remember much, but I now know how he was killed." "Based on a dream?" "No. Based on this GPS device."

"I don't understand." "In my dream, I thought your father was dead. In fact he was alive." "But you saw his body?" "Yes." "Then he's dead."

"In my dream I was uncertain if he was dead or alive. It's like this GPS. We can't be certain it will get us to Police HQ." "We're here."

It was true. We were at the entrance to Police Headquarters. "How?" I asked. "I do have some idea of how to drive in this city, GPS or not."

"Wait," said Regi, "I want to clear the air." "About what?" "When we met I said you were an idiot." "That's OK. I get that all the time."

"It was a thoughtless comment. I didn't know you then. Now that I know you better I'm afraid you really are an idiot. I want to apologize."

"No apology is necessary. In my line you develop a shell or you don't last." "But how do you ever solve a crime when you're dumb as toast?"

"Technique. When all else fails, investigative technique pulls you through." "Well, it all seems miraculous to me." "Yes, I guess it would."

"If you do solve a crime it's a miracle?" "I mean to the uninitiated any sufficiently advanced technology is indistinguishable from magic."

Chapter 15

City Morgue

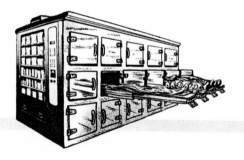

After the unusual architecture I'd encountered in this case, it was a comfort to return to the surplus washroom tile ambiance of Police HQ.

I flashed my cellphone badge as we walked past the front desk. "Hey Arkaby!" said the Desk Sergeant "Where have you been?" "Solving crimes."

My standard reply always left everyone laughing. "This is a material witness. We're going to the Morgue." "The Morgue is that way." "Right."

The City Morgue was three levels down. After everything that had happened, I needed to see Granger's body parts again with my own eyes.

At the start of this case the Coroner told me he had 3 1/2 other victims just like Granger back at the Morgue. I needed to see them too.

"Are you ready?" I asked Regi. "I was born ready." she replied. "I mean are you ready to view your father's remains?" "Oh...I'm not sure."

"Do you think he suffered much?" "Yes, I do." "But he's now in a better place?" "I doubt it." "Does his death have any meaning?" "None."

Regi had it right. Nothing could be gained by brooding over the dead. Or waiting for an elevator at Police Headquarters. We took the stairs.

As we reached the Morgue entrance the smells of cured meats and formaldehyde filled the air. "Phew!" said Regi. "Is this the right floor?"

"How did you think a morgue smelled?" "Like death. I get the overwhelming fumes that take your breath away. What's with the pickle juice?"

"So Oscar Mayer smells make sense but not formaldehyde?" "Do you have any idea what's in salami?" "Let's find out." I pushed open the doors.

The Deputy Coroner sat at the front desk, attacking the bow end of a sub sandwich. "We're here to view the deceased." I said "Where's Doc?"

"He stepped out." the DC said through a mouthful of sub. "Come back another time." "That's OK. Just point me toward the refrigerator room."

"Who are you here for?" "Granger." "No Granger here." "White male, average build?" "Doesn't ring a bell." "Brought in Tuesday?" "Nope."

"Cut in half?" "I would have noticed." "I was with Doc at the crime scene Tuesday night!" "Well he isn't here." "Is there another morgue?"

"This is the only place they bring the bodies." Regi stepped in. "Are you saying you've misplaced my father?" "I'm saying we never had him."

"Show me." said Regi. "Show you what?" "What you've got." "I know Detective Arkaby here. Who are you?" "I'm Regna Granger. Show me."

The Deputy Coroner led us to the next room. We stood before a long bank of body drawers. "I should warn you, we get some weird cases here."

He opened the first drawer. "This is 'John Doe'. We don't know his real name. Not Granger, I'm guessing." "Not Granger." I confirmed.

A woman's body lay in the next drawer. "This is 'Jane Doe'. We don't know yet who she is." "Wrong sex anyway and all in one piece." I said.

"All these Does." said Regi "Do you have any body in your system with a verified identity?" "Of course. We're coming to them." said the DC.

He opened the next drawer. "Also John Doe." "Another unknown?" "No. That's actually his name." He closed the drawer. "This next one's odd."

He opened the fourth drawer. Inside lay Snap, Crackle and Pop from the Rice Krispies box. "We think this is the work of a cereal killer."

Stacked in the next drawer were twisted, ruined sheets of aluminum. "We believe this unfortunate situation is due to a home siding maniac."

Regi said "All you have here are some redundant unknowns, several low fiber celebrities and assorted building supplies?" "That's right."

Past the last drawer was a locked door. "What's in there?" "That's a deep freeze storage room." "Can you open it?" Just then the phone rang.

"I've been called on a case" the DC said, hanging up the phone. "We're not finished." I said. "You'll have to wait for my boss to return."

I watched the DC prepare his kit. "I still need to know three things. First, what's in the freezer?" "Doc will show you when he gets back."

"While we wait, I'll check the Coroner's Log. Is there a computer I can use?" "Sure. Use that one over there. Just sign in as yourself."

"Third, are you going to finish that sub?" "Arkaby!" said Regi. "Yes I am." said the DC. "Why?" "I haven't eaten since this case started."

"I'm so hungry I could eat the possibly poisoned tapioca in my pocket. You know how much I hate tapioca." "I'm taking the sub with me."

The Deputy Coroner left with his crime kit and his sub sandwich. Regi said "You go do whatever you have to do. I'll go buy you a candy bar."

Regi went in search of a vending machine. Logging onto the computer I realized that I had a chance to access Granger's Twitter account.

I pulled out the paper B had given me. Though smeared with tapioca, I could still make out the letters of Granger's password printed on it.

'Ullhodturdenweirmudgaardgringnirurdrmolnirfenrirlukkilokkibau gimandodrrerinsurtkrinmgernrackinarockar.' I rejoiced that I still had it.

It took a while to type his password into Twitter exactly. Where was a copy of 'A Skeleton Key to Finnegans Wake' when you really needed it?

I had seen Granger's final two entries: His "aaaaa..." that was either a death cry or his finger stuck on the 'a' key; his tapioca distress.

As I clicked to open his Twitter history I heard footsteps behind me. "I hope you brought me a Snickers Bar" I said without turning around.

I felt something hard press against my back. "Is that a Butterfingers or are you glad to see me?" "Don't turn around." said a husky voice.

"Do you really think you can scare me with a candy bar?" "No, you idiot. This is a gun. A 'real one with real bullets'." I knew that voice.

"You! It was you who called me while I was driving and sent me into a multitasking fugue!" "Yes." "Why?" "You were getting too close."

"Rachel Granger hadn't missed her honey 'til you showed up." "You fiend! What did you do to her bees?" "Nothing. She was already bee-reft."

"You sabotaged the car?" "That car had several well-known safety issues. I just helped them along." "I know someone who wants to meet you."

"What about the explosive device under the dashboard that I diffused?" "What you actually did was disconnect the self-heating cup holder."

"You made the Wright Tower water pipe burst? You tipped the reporters on my location? You sent the tapioca to B?" "All part of the plan."

"And all the Twitter system crashes and Fail Whales?" "No, that was the Twitter administrators rising to their own level of incompetence."

"I don't get it." "I delayed you so I could expunge Granger's Twitter account." "I get that. Why deliver the pizza to Regi's hospital room?"

"I was tracking your GPS coordinates from your cell phone and they were off a little." "That one little thing you couldn't get right?"

"You've been a step ahead of me this entire case. How did you do it?" "It was easy. You tweeted all of your activities. You're a real Twit."

"So you're my sole Twitter follower? You're 'HelloKitty1781'?" "Yes." "Under other circumstances I'd be delighted to meet you." "Ditto."

"Why reveal yourself now?" "You were supposed to be in surgery at Body Parts 'R' Us and out of commission a while. You've mucked things up."

"You have to admit that I was just a few clues shy of nailing you." "You wouldn't know a clue if it came along and bit you on the ankle."

The door swung open and Regi walked in. "They didn't have anything healthy so I got...YOU!" "Regi, meet the City Coroner. I call him 'Doc'."

"I don't care what you call him," said Regi "don't you know who he is?" "Who?" "Arkaby, meet A." "A?" "Yes" "B's older brother?" "The same."

"Doc is A?" "Yes!" "A is the Coroner?" "Evidently." Regi's disclosure hit me like a denial-of-service attack. My systems began to shut down.

That's why B looked familiar in the Tunnel Tower! He resembled his brother A not Granger! B probably wasn't sleeping with his mother either.

As Coroner, A controlled the evidence and subverted my entire investigation. Blocking me at every turn, A was my own personal Fail Whale.

It made perfect sense. No wonder A bested me! He must have seen my Twitter posts as manna from heaven. Maybe I should switch to Facebook.

A motioned Regi to join me. "Why's A pointing a gun at you?" she asked. "A killed your father." "A?" "Yes." "B's older brother?" "The same."

"It was A all along?" "Yes!" "Excuse me" said A. "One minute." said Regi "Really, A did it?" "Evidently." "You're kidding." "I wish I were."

"Hey! I'm standing right here!" "WILL YOU WAIT?" Regi and I said. A placed the gun barrel against my nose. "I'm pressed for time." A said.

"You gall the shods." I said "Do you thig you gan ged away with this id the middle of a bolice statiod?" "Absolutely. You're going on ice."

A removed his gun. I needed to know three things: WHY did A kill Granger? HOW did he do it? WHAT was the deal with the tapioca? Seriously.

"What about all the tapioca? Was it just to get to me?" "No. It was an unanticipated consequence." A's words reassured me. I'm not sure why.

"Violence is the last resort of the incompetent." "Whoever said that wasn't the one holding the gun. You still don't know how I did it."

"Any fool can see you bisected Granger with a katana while riding a speeding motorbike." "That's ridiculous. You watch too much CSI-Miami."

"How then?" "You know that Granger started out in horse racing?" "Yes. He was the first entrant to win the Kentucky Derby without a horse."

<hr/>

"My father wasn't a racehorse!" said Regi. "Once you run the Kentucky Derby it's in your blood." "What has that got to do with his murder?"

"During his last cloning operation I stitched Granger up with fast-dissolving sutures. They disintegrated before he healed completely."

"Then I set his ring tone to play 'Call To Post.' When I called him his bottom half took off down the track and left his top half behind."

Of course. It made perfect sense. In my dream Granger's two halves couldn't agree which way to go. Reality Granger faced a similar choice.

Befuddled by toxic tapioca and pulled in two directions at once, Granger suffered a split personality. A had committed the perfect crime.

"I've doctored our records and hidden Granger with some of his cloned spare parts in this freezer. You'll join him soon to vanish forever."

"At the crime scene the other day you said you had 3 1/2 other victims 'just like' Granger. Were you referring to his clone parts?" "Yes."

"So You 'disappear' the entrepreneur, scientist and racehorse, but can you silence Granger the podcast mime?" "Out of sight, out of mime."

I had to admit, A had me stumped. He had gone to a lot of trouble to kill Granger in an especially gruesome way and for no apparent reason.

"Did you kill Granger to save Body Parts R Us from dissolution?" "I don't care about that." "You wanted to collect concierge fees?" "Nope."

"You were in love with Rachel Lehcar and killed Granger to get him out of the way?" "He was already out of the way and I don't love Rachel."

"You killed Granger to triumph over your consonant siblings?" "Not even close." "Maybe it was an accident?" "No. It was well planned."

Regi spoke up. "I know. You killed my father because he would never consent to our marriage." I looked at Regi. "You were seeing A?"

"No! It's the only explanation left." She turned to A. "I'd never marry you under any circumstances." "I didn't ask." "You're a monster!"

"Take it easy Arkaby." said Regi "If asked I would not accept and if wedded I would not serve." "He's still a monster!" "Well, sure."

A unlocked the door to the freezer. I had run out of ideas and it looked like time as well. That forced me to ask A one final question.

"Why did you kill Granger?" "It was necessary." "Murder is never necessary." "It was in this case. Granger took his augmentation too far."

A said "'And this man is now become a god and Cassius is a wretched creature and must bend his body, if Caesar carelessly but nod on him.'"

"Do you know that quote?" A asked. "No." A tried again: "'And therefore think him as a serpent's egg ...And kill him in the shell.'"

"The original Star Trek?" "No, you idiot! Julius Caesar!" "You killed my father because of an orange drink?" "I think he means the salad."

"You killed my father because of a salad?" "That's from Shakespeare, not a menu. I killed him because he dared think of himself as a god."

"I can quote Shakespeare too: 'A man's a man for a' that. For a' that, and a' that.'" "That's Robert Burns." "Not Shakespeare?" "No."

"So...to stop Granger from becoming a god, you made the god-like decision to end his life." "Yes." "You don't see a flaw in your thinking?"

"What flaw?" "You've applied a 1st century solution to a 21st century problem." "My only problem is you, and that's about to be resolved."

We entered the freezer. Two black body bags lay on a table in the center. Shelves along the wall held bags with various Granger clone parts.

A said "I'll leave you two here and let nature take its course." "Thanks for the offer, but I think we'll be too busy freezing to death."

Regi said "You killed my father because of words in a play?" "Not the words, the idea." "What idea?" "The idea I could kill your father."

A shut the door and we plunged into icy darkness. After a moment the door opened again. A said "One thing more. Hand over your cell phone."

Chapter 16

Frozen POPs

"   "

"   "

Robert K. Blechman

Not much time. I'm Police Detective Arkaby. We have been
locked in the freezer at the City Morgue by the murderer of
Willum Granger.

I'm trapped in here with Willum Granger's frozen remains, with
Regi Granger, his live daughter and with 3 1/2 sets of his cloned
body parts.

Regi has warmed up her dead father's dead phone in a way I can't
describe and the power came on. There's no phone service but I've
got WIFI.

I'm public tweeting with Granger's dying phone. We know A is his
killer. If we can't get out of this freezer, he'll make a clean
getaway.

Help us escape! Use the hashtag #freezerburn and suggest a way
out of this freezer. Or you could call upstairs and tell the Desk
Sergeant.

Damn, its cold! McLuhan said the stimulating shock of new
technology causes a numbing of mind and body. This is especially
true of freezers.

Fingers and toes already numb. Signal getting weaker. Shutting
down to conserve phone battery. I'll look for Twitter responses
later.

"   "

126

RT @TwitsteryFan: I've been following your Twitstery since the beginning! This is really exciting! #freezerburn /OK. That didn't help.

RT @NotLockedIn: You got yourself locked in the freezer and the killer is escaping? What a dumbass! #freezerburn /No trolls please!

RT @JoyceScholar: Ineluctable modality of the visible: at least that if no more, thought through my eyes. #freezerburn /Agenbite of inwit!

RT @SoccerMom: Chill out man! You've got the babe on ice. All you need now is some brew! #freezerburn /You don't sound like a soccermom.

RT Sweet! Lady Gaga wrote a song about @freezerburns! http://bit.ly/clUVGk Ok not really. But the song is called "Freezerburn" /Not helping!

RT @ModelMediaEcologist: McLuhan meant a technology-induced psychic numbness, not a physical one. #freezerburn /Point taken, but not helping!

RT @Houdini: Every freezer has an idiot's latch. YOU should have no trouble finding it. You can't be locked in. #freezerburn /I'll look.

I looked for a latch. Either I'm a real idiot, or this freezer doesn't have one. "Could be both" said Regi. The battery is holding for now.

I'll record what I can for later tweeting. After A locked us in, I found a light switch by the door. Regi and I huddled to conserve heat.

"I wish we'd met under different circumstances." Regi said. "Yes" I replied "being freeze-dried in a morgue isn't the best first date ever."

"Date? I mean I wish you were a rich industrialist or a celebrity and that I...well, I was the same as I am." "I also wish you were the same."

"What difference does it make?" "Imagine the headlines: 'Regi Granger Found in Freezer with A-Rod' or 'Granger Heir In Icy Trump Embrace.'"

We huddled closer together against the cold. Suddenly Regi pulled back. "What's that? We're freezing to death and you're aroused?" "Sorry."

"Great! Instead of a hot superstar, I've got a horny cop. When they find us the headline will be 'Ice Queen Found Frozen With Stiff Dick.'"

"And I wish this freezer had a phone and that I had a warmer top and snow boots." "What did you say?" "About my boots? "No the other thing."

"I wish I had a warmer top?" "The other other thing." "I wish this freezer had a phone?" "Yes that's it." "Well, it doesn't. Look around."

Maybe there was a phone here. I went to the table with the body bags. Unzipping one bag I struck pay dirt! But why was the bag full of dirt?

Maybe that was how A planned to make a clean getaway. In the other bag were Granger's remains and...his cell phone! Both were frozen solid.

I brought it over to Regi. "Sometimes a phone's dead battery retains a residual charge. If we can thaw this out, we might get a signal."

I rubbed the phone between my hands, but they were too cold to make a difference. I put the phone in my armpit but that was just unpleasant.

"Give me the phone" said Regi "and one of those surgical gloves. Now turn around and promise me you won't peek." "What are you going to do?"

"Just trust me. Now turn around." I heard Regi slip the surgical glove over the phone and then silence punctuated by some muffled grunts.

"I think that did it." Regi peeled off the glove and handed me the phone. It worked! I had no phone service, but I picked up a WIFI signal.

I tweeted my initial calls for help and then shut down the phone. As we huddled together again I thought about baseball. "Now we wait."

"That was an experience I don't want to repeat." said Regi. "What did you do with the phone?" I asked. "I put it in a warm place." "What!"

"Where exactly did you put the phone?" "In my mouth. Where did you think I put it?" "Never mind." I thought about baseball some more.

"Freezing isn't such a bad thing." said Regi. "How so?" "We fall asleep and awaken in the 25th century with Ted Williams and Walt Disney."

"And then we can time travel back to where we are now and save ourselves." "That's not likely." "Why? You don't believe in time travel?"

"First, Disney was cremated. Second, if we come back to save ourselves, then we'll never freeze to death and awaken in the 25th century."

"Third, if we triumph over causation by time traveling, no one could ever be convicted of a misdeed. Crime detection would become obsolete."

"With no crimes to solve I'd be out of work." "We have to freeze to death to save your job?" "I'm afraid so." "That's really selfish of you"

Regi looked over to the table. "Are those body bags my father?" "Just one. The other's a dirt bag." "Who?" "No one. Just a bag of dirt."

"What do you think A planned to do with all my father's clone parts?" "We'll ask him when we get out of here." I turned the phone back on.

None of the tweets helped. After looking for an idiot's latch I rechecked Twitter. There was one final reply or perhaps I was hallucinating:

RT @IGSDir: Don't fight the cold. Go into suspended animation, emerge in 2410, use a time machine to go back to where you were/Wow! Déjà vu!

"That's it?" Regi asked. "That's all they twote." "Twote? Not tweeted?" "No. Twote." Regi looked at me. "OK" she said "Let's m-make l-love."

"You may think 'twote' is not a real word, but I would argue...I'm sorry. What d-did you say?" "I s-said 'Let's do it.'" "Huh?" "Make love."

"N-NOW you have a ch-change of heart?" "If we're g-going to die anyway, we should go out with a b-bang." "Or in my c-case, a w-whimper."

"Are y-you sure?" "Sure? I just offered to hook up in front of my father's corpsicle. I'm fr-freezing. I m-may not be in my right m-mind."

Despite the freezer's bitter cold, Regi's lips were surprisingly warm and reminded me of a petite madeleine soaked in hot lime-flower tea.

Memories flooded back; a shudder ran through my whole body, and I stopped, intent upon the extraordinary changes that were taking place.

I remembered the streets of my childhood town and visits to my ailing aunt who invariably called me "Bruce" even though that isn't my name.

During one fateful visit I locked myself in her walk-in freezer and would still be there but for her fondness for frozen tapioca pudding.

After a time my Aunt's maid, Francoise, opened the freezer to retrieve some tapioca and discovered me, tapioca cartons scattered all around.

"What a dreadful thing for parents to have a child like this!" Francoise exclaimed as she lifted me up and carried me off to be thawed out.

Now I was locked in a freezer again. I thought about how there wasn't any tapioca in here. That wasn't reassuring. I kissed Regi again.

"So Arkaby," said Regi as we kissed, "do you have a first name?" I brushed back a strand of her golden hair. "You couldn't pronounce it."

The freezer door flew open. "Not yet!" I shouted. Outside were Brynhildur Cathedra and her fiancé, X. Next to them stood X's brother, A.

A's wrists were cuffed. "We're in time" said Brynhildur as she and X rushed in and half carried, half walked Regi and me out of the freezer.

Outside were Rachel Lehcar, B, Dot and Dash, the BP'R'U Concierge, the Deputy Coroner, the Desk Sergeant, and half the city police force.

I had no feeling in my legs but managed to stand upright and pull up my pants. "Lock yourself in the freezer again?" asked the Desk Sergeant.

I tried to say "What are you doing here?" but I was so frozen it came out as "Mmmfff?" "Don't talk." "Jusht walk." said Dot and Dash.

Rachel Lehcar wrapped a blanket around Regi. B handed me my cell phone. "Y rlly r sht fr brns dmb fck rnt y?" he said. "H-h-how?" I grunted.

"B hypothesized about your intelligence" explained X. "I got th-that. How did you find us?" "Ms. Cathedra here alerted us." said the DC.

"Thanks to her we captured A before he could escape." I hadn't seen Brynhildur since the flooded left Wright Tower. "How d-did you know?"

"As part of my M.O.B.Y.D.I.C.K. activities I monitor all social media with a scanbot that flags any occurrence of the term 'Fail Whale'."

"The scanbot alerted me to a tweet about A being your own personal Fail Whale. I realized you were in trouble and gathered everyone else."

"Thank you Brynhildur. I couldn't have succeeded without your help." Brynhildur laughed. "Succeeded? I guess Winston Churchill was right."

"Churchill?" "He said 'Success is going from failure to failure without a loss of enthusiasm.'" "Well, I'm lucky to have so many friends."

"And I'm touched that all of you came to rescue us." "Regi is my daughter." said Rachel Lehcar "I've lost my bees. I couldn't lose her too."

"I wouldn't miss it for all the tea in China." said X, grinning. "I came to reclaim the clone parts A pilfered." said Dot. "Damn" said Dash.

That was one thing I didn't get. I turned to A. "Why do you have 3 1/2 Granger clones?" "They were there for Granger's benefit, not mine."

"Aren't they spares to patch Granger if you didn't succeed in killing him?" "I took an oath 'First, do no harm.'" "Second, cover your ass?"

"Prove it." A said. "Why didn't you delete Granger's Twitter entries?" "I was too busy chasing you." "Who's the twit now?" They led him off.

The Body Parts 'R' Us Concierge stepped up. "This is for you" he said, handing me a large white envelope. "What is it, a reward?" I asked.

"No. It's your hospital bill. $40,000 plus extra printing." "Thanks." The crowd thinned out. I went up to where Regi stood with her mother.

We hugged. "I think I'll miss you most of all" I said. "If you do" she whispered "use your phone." How did she know about my girlfriend app?

"To call me?" "Oh." "You know how to do that don't you? You put your lips together and blow." "Huh?" "Assuming you have voice dialing." "Ah."

I was left with the Desk Sergeant and the Deputy Coroner. "I guess I've solved the murder of Willum Granger." "Not really" replied the DC.

"We can hold A for putting you and Ms. Granger in the deep freeze, but we still have no hard evidence proving he killed Granger."

"Hard evidence?" I reached into my pocket for the tapioca, which had frozen solid, and handed it to the DC. "The proof is in the pudding."

About the Author

Robert K. Blechman is not a cartoonist. —That's Robert O.— Robert K. was born at the start of the turbulent 1950's and spent the first 17 years of his life in a house on the western boundary between Maryland and the District of Columbia, that is, on the demarcation line determining voting and non-voting citizenship. He graduated from the University of Chicago with a BA in English Literature and went on to earn an MBA in finance and a Ph.D. in Media Ecology from New York University.

During the Viet Nam War Dr. Blechman received a moderately high draft lottery number and so avoided military service. He was gassed once during an anti-war protest in Chicago, but otherwise emerged unscathed.

Until recently he held a senior technology position at a major medical school. He has worked a variety of jobs, including summers as a counselor at Camp Zakelo in Harrison, Maine, and several semesters as an adjunct professor of media studies at Fordham University.

In the course of his corporate career Dr. Blechman has held management positions at iconic national institutions and has experienced a major bankruptcy, a major merger, downsizing, resizing and rightsizing. He could write a book. He was triaged from Columbia University Medical Center when royalty money from the Axel patents dried up; expelled from the New York City Board of Education on pedagogical differences; debited at PricewaterhouseCoopers LLP by his counterpart after a major merger; remaindered at HarperCollins Publishers during a change in senior management and deconstructed when Olympia & York Real Estate Management went belly up. All things being equal, Dr. Blechman looks forward to retirement.

Besides the present volume, Dr. Blechman looks to his three children, Alexander, Sara and Eliana to validate his time spent on this planet. Otherwise it's pretty much a wash.

Dr. Blechman continues to tweet at RKBs_Twitstery, discusses his Media Ecological musings and speculations at his blog, "A Model Media Ecologist" at www.robertkblechman.blogspot.com and is hard at work on a follow-up novel to Executive Severance.

NeoPoiesis: *a new way of making*

1) in ancient Greece, poiesis referred to the process of making: creation - production - organization - formation - causation

2) a process that can be physical and spiritual, biological and intellectual, artistic and technological, material and teleological, efficient and formal

3) a means of modifying the environment and a method of organizing the self, the making of art and music and poetry, the fashioning of memory and history and philosophy, the construction of perception and expression and reality

4) an independent publisher with a steadfast goal to print and promote outstanding poets, writers and artists that reflect the creative drive and spirit of the new electronic landscape

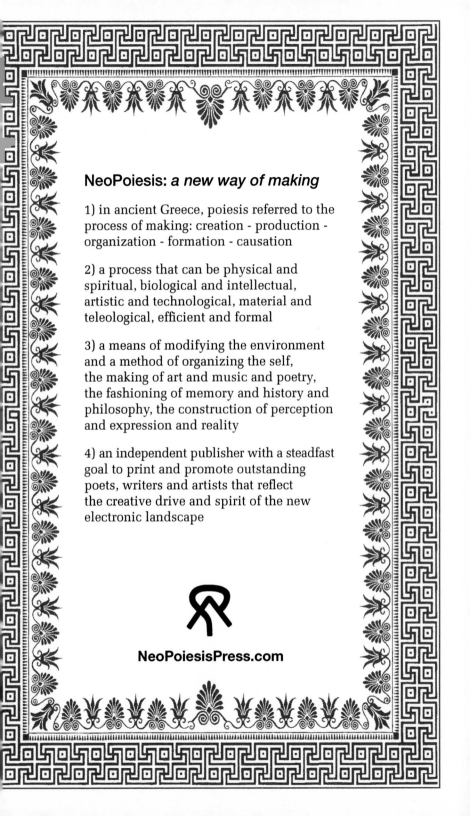

NeoPoiesisPress.com

CPSIA information can be obtained at www.ICGtesting.com
Printed in the USA
BVOW011331080112

280000BV00002B/1/P

9 780983 274759